To Jan

FATE & FLUX

A STEAMPUNK ADVENTURE

Enjoy!

PATRICK DUGAN

To my family who I'd be lost without.

"Do I need to incinerate your assistant to prove how serious I take this matter?" Magus Crimshaw, the Luxor family's newly raised wizard, threatened the forge master for the third time. His family owned lands to the west of Bradenbridge where his father served our patron, Usorin, Lord Magus of Terralon.

I stayed down behind the bellows where I could see and hear without making my presence known. Even as a journeyman blacksmith, staying out of a Magus' way was a good idea.

Ruari, the master of the forge, ducked his head just like he'd taught us. The magi controlled powers far beyond anything I'd ever understand and they were a finicky bunch.

"Magus, I'm sorry as I can be, but Lord Usorin has set my hand to this project before any of his retainers'. You might speak to Chancellor Eamon, as he is keeper of the books."

Crimshaw spit into the dirt.

"Grovel to a commoner? I am a Magus, and if you want my business, you'll do as I ask. I want those iron collars in seven days' time or I'll have your head on my mantel."

"Is that so?" A voice came from the front of the forge. Ruari dropped to one knee immediately.

Crimshaw froze when he heard it. He turned and knelt in the direction of the new arrival.

"I meant no disrespect, my Lord."

Lord Magus Usorin, strolled into sight, followed by his brown metal golem. Usorin's long brown hair, pulled back at his neck, was the same color as his goatee. His dark red robes hung just above the dirt as he addressed Crimshaw.

"Ruari is my blacksmith and does my bidding. I allow my underlings to use his services, if he has time. What right do you possess that allows you to threaten my man?"

"None, my Lord," Crimshaw whispered, his head lower than before. "I was in error, please forgive me."

The golem held out a scabbarded sword to him. Usorin's eye flickered to the sword and then back to the kneeling mage.

I'd have laughed at the pompous windbag if I wasn't scared out of my wits. No one laughed at Usorin. He had a reputation for being easily offendable and killed when others would scold. The people of Bradenbridge treaded lightly around the Lord Magus, and for good reason.

With a scraping noise, Usorin pulled the blade from the scabbard the golem held and brandished it in front of Crimshaw's pale face. The darkened steel reflected no light. I'd never seen a flame blade in person before.

"The next time I find you threatening one of my retainers, I will have your head. Get out of my sight."

Crimshaw bolted out of the forge, robes trailing behind him.

The golem cackled at the fleeing mage. Only the most powerful of magi conjured golems to do their bidding; this one had been created in the image of a miniature man. He wore a wide brimmed bowler hat and a thick mustache that appeared to be made of metal. Usorin ignored the golem, focusing on the master blacksmith.

"Thank you, Lord Magus," Ruari said, his eyes on the dirt.

"I will not have the lesser houses thinking they can threaten what is mine. I have need of you, Ruari."

"I am at your service, always, my Lord."

"My flame blade is not working properly. I need you to address the issue."

Ruari stood, eyes still downcast. "May I have the sword?"

Usorin swung the blade, stopping it just short of the master blacksmith's neck.

"It will kill people who betray me even without the flame. Won't it, Ruari?"

"Yes, my Lord, though only a fool would betray you." Ruari's head hadn't moved an inch as he spoke.

The Lord Magus reversed the sword with practiced ease and presented the pommel to the master smith. Ruari took the sword and retreated deeper into the shop. I scrambled from my hiding spot to help him. He waved me over as I entered the back of the smithy.

There were three portions to the Blacksmith shop. On the right side of the shop stood the farriers section since it butted up to a horse corral. The bunkhouse and Ruari's home sat behind this section. The main portion of the smithy is where he built metal works, both useful and ornate. Two large coal forges stood behind anvils and other tools of the trade. Back behind the forges, Ruari had a small area for more delicate projects or ones involving expensive materials. This part of the shop had walls on the sides to keep towns-folk from nosing about.

"Keep your voice down, Quinn." Ruari chose a tool from its hanging spot on the wall. He pried open the pommel cap, and with a long pair of tweezers, removed a piece of what looked like iron. "Get me a piece of alarium and be quick."

3

I ran into the store room where we stocked extra ingots and metals from around the kingdom that we used to make everything from blades to high priced tools for the local craftsmen. I moved a panel in the wall and unlocked the steel safe with the key I wore around my neck. I removed a glass vial containing a piece of alarium, and it sparkled as it hit the light. Ruari never told me why we kept the supply on hand; just gave me a key in case something happened to him and swore me to secrecy. I returned with the metal.

"I thought the flame blades were magic?" I asked quietly. Magi were notoriously closed lipped about their magic and didn't respond kindly to commoners asking questions.

"The alarium stores the magic they funnel into it. Sometimes, the metal cracks and won't hold no proper magic. Leaks it out, sure enough." Ruari opened the vial, extracted the metal, and deposited it in the pommel before resealing it. "Never let the stuff touch your skin. If it does, cut the skin off fast or it will kill you. Wait here."

I'd heard the same warning on the rare occasions we used alarium. Usorin trusted his most senior people with the material, but only the magi could power the stuff since no one else possessed magic. I moved to the side and watched Usorin pace back and forth impatiently. Ruari returned to his master, holding the sword out to the Lord Magus as he knelt before him. With a swipe, the blade burst into light, flames licking the edges of the steel. Rumor was the sword had cut through plate armor.

"Excellent," Usorin said as he eyed the flame blade, and slid it back into its scabbard with a faint hiss. "I will have my furnace in two days?"

"Yes, Lord Usorin. The boys have been working round the clock to make sure it's done right."

Usorin sniffed. "As they should. I don't want to be disappointed."

I saw Ruari stiffen. "Nor I, my Lord."

Usorin pivoted on his heel and strode out of the forge without another word. His metal golem bowed stiffly and followed his master out.

I moved to stand next to Ruari, letting out the nervous breath I'd been holding. Even though I was a journeyman blacksmith, I had no desire to deal with wizards.

"Boy, he's strung tighter than a lute."

"Keep your voice down, Quinn," Ruari said, glancing around the forge. "Insultin' a wizard will get you burnt alive regardless if you're a smith or not."

I nodded. I'd been with the master blacksmith since I was seven, as close as I could tell. My ma had died, and I'd been given to Ruari to train up. He was the father I never had, or at least knew of.

"I've been with you long enough to know that, Master. In fifteen years, I've learned a lot more than my way around the forge."

"That you have." Ruari mopped his face with a rag he kept tucked under his belt. "How is the coal chamber comin' for Usorin's furnace?"

"Done, as far as I can tell. Once Tur finishes up the supports, we'll be ready to go."

Ruari had a reputation for crafting pieces that all the wizards wanted. Usorin commissioned a furnace to heat his keep, and Ruari had designed and built it. With autumn ending soon, Usorin was pushing hard for the work to be finished so he didn't have to rely on fireplaces and stoves for heat. Knowing the Lord Magus, he'd be gloating to his vassals all winter long. Well, if it worked.

Over the summer, Usorin's carpenters had created wooden ducts that would carry warm air from the furnace to the main rooms of the keep. Ruari's blower system of cogs, gears, and a massive set of fan blades were housed over the furnace where the steam generator would push the air through. My contribution consisted of a large, banded iron trough lined with steel that would contain the burning coal. The lining ensured the coal fire couldn't burn through the trough.

"Well, he better be done, 'cause in two days we need to put it in place," Ruari said. "We should load up the finished pieces tonight so we don't have to do it all at once. Go get the lads and we'll see about loadin' the burner."

I ran from the metal works and into the farrier shop. All blacksmiths apprenticed here before Ruari would let them start their journeyman training with him. Some never made it for lack of talent or wits; any competent smith could turn out a decent shoe, but not everyone could build the contraptions that Ruari designed.

"Bran, Tur!" I shouted over the clang of hammers striking hot iron, "Get the boys, we need to load up the wagons."

Bran looked up from the anvil where he was bending a shoe into shape over the horn. He towered over most men and was broader than any two.

"I've got to get this gelding shod for Magus Ailene. She's been waitin' on it."

"And who promised it to her today, 'fore all the others?" Tur asked as he crossed over to the anvil where Bran worked. He wore his long, brown hair back in a tail to keep it out of his face. Unlike the massive Bran, Tur was strong without being a large man. Tur caught my eye, shaking his head at the futility of chasing a Magus. "You know she's got no feelins fer a commoner, right?"

Bran's face glowed like the metal he shaped.

"I know, you stupid git. The gelding would have turned up lame without a new shoe and the Lord Magus would hear about it, is all."

I checked his work, and it was barely passable. Bran's

arms outran his skill by a mile. He could crush your hand to pulp but could barely manage a good horseshoe.

"Alarik, come finish this shoe."

A young, spindly teen walked over and used the proffered tongs to get the shoe.

"Magus is waitin' on it, so do it good," Bran said as the boy took it. The boy's face twisted as he looked at the mildly mangled piece of iron.

I holler over the noise. "Bran, go see if we can borrow a couple porters from the hosteller. We'll need the extra hands." I waited until the big man was out of earshot. "Throw it in the slag pile and get a fresh piece."

Alarik smiled back. "Thanks, Quinn. Wasn't sure how I'd fix that mess."

I winked at him. "Make it quick. You don't want Bran to realize we threw out his piece."

"Yep." Alarik already had a new piece of iron in the coal and pumped the bellows to get it up to temperature. Kid would make a good smith someday.

The sun warmed my back as I headed to the wagons. Tur and Ruari were pointing and gesturing at the furnace as I approached.

"Is there a problem?" I asked as I approached the two men.

"No, just thinkin' about how to best load the monster," the master smith said. "I know you built it right, but she's a beast."

I smirked. One of the things Ruari looked for in a journeyman was ingenuity. I'd foreseen this issue and took steps to avoid it.

"Well, if you look, there are four pass-throughs on the bottom. If we take the old axles in the back, we can rig wheels on and have the horses drag the thing to the keep. I even put a jump seat on the front for the driver."

Tur whistled softly. "That's a good one. Never thought of it, myself."

Ruari clapped me on the back. "That's why Quinn is the journeyman, he works with his head as much as his arms. When my time comes, he'll be takin' over the forge."

All I'd ever wanted to do was make Ruari proud of me and never wonder why he'd taken on a scrawny orphan as an apprentice. Today, I accomplished that goal.

Bran walked up with three beefy men in tow. They all stopped and stared. I heard a few muttered curses.

"Shit, we've got to move that?"

Ruari snorted. "No, we need to get the other pieces in the wagon. They'll be heavy enough. Quinn, go ahead and get the axles in place and see if it works."

Smiling the whole way, I carried the heavy iron axles over and affixed them to the furnace. The wheels slid on with some effort, but after a couple of hours, they were all fitted and ready to test. Ropes came out from under the piece and were tied to the beams that supported the iron furnace.

Bran and Tur helped me pull the supports out, and, with a loud thump, the furnace settled onto the wheels. Ruari was all smiles as he examined the improvised wagon.

"That's a clever bit of work. I think we can call it a day, boys." The master smith wiped his sweaty face before tucking the cloth away again.

Tur approached me as I studied my handiwork.

"There's a duel up at the arena. Since we're done early, let's go watch."

I shook my head. "Nah, you go on. I'm gonna work on the knife I'm forging for master Ruari."

Duels were a waste of time. I hated watching cocky wizards fighting over some insult or other stupid thing. Nobody died, and if you were unlucky enough to run into the loser afterwards, they might blast you just for looking at them wrong.

Tur shrugged, smirking at me as he teased. He was the older brother I never had. Always up to mischief and half the time getting me wrapped up in it.

"Suit yerself. Gael told me Emma was going. Maybe I'll just entertain both of them myself."

"You didn't mention Emma was coming along." Emma was beautiful and kind. I'd taken a fancy to her, long ago, but lacked the courage to talk to her much.

Tur nodded sagely. "Wouldn't do to be out with Gael alone, or at least that's what she tells me."

"Since, it'd be helping you out, I better come with you. Plus, I need to keep you out of trouble."

An early day. Seeing Emma. Could things get any better?

2

W e walked along with the townsfolk headed to see the spectacle of the Wizard's Duel; farmers brought in their whole families to see a duel. The arena stood in the center of town, and on our way there, we passed vendors selling everything imaginable: fruits and vegetables, cured meat, breads. Small trinkets of bone and metal sat next to a woman telling fortunes, and an alchemist sold cures for anything that might ail you.

Maids and house matrons carried their purchases in wicker baskets, younger children clung to their mama's skirts, and older children ran ahead and were called after. Horse-drawn wagons ran down the center of the street, delivering supplies or hauling goods to the broker shops at the far end of town. Wealthy merchants had shops where wizards of all level shopped for luxuries, I could only guess.

We reached the commoners' entrance and paid a copper each to go in. The tunnel led to the lower level seats where most of the lower classes sat. After the heat of the forge, the cool fall night was a welcome respite. Duels were always done after dark so the wizards could show off their magic.

Tur pushed past a couple of men at the end of the tunnel. I followed as he took the stairs two at a time to where he'd told the girls to meet us. I'd noticed over the years that his taste in women erred on the larger side. Gael was stout, her long, dark hair pulled back in a twin style to Tur's. I froze when I saw Emma sitting next to her. She wore a blue cloth over her dark hair and a light blue smock. Emma worked as a seamstress for one of the ladies of Lord Usorin's family, a position that placed her slightly above commoner status. Her green eyes caught mine as I stood there like a piece of iron gripped in a vise. She was lovely in a way I couldn't define.

Tur returned down the stairs to where I stood and smacked me on the arm. "You've gotta walk all the way up to talk to her." He grinned from ear to ear. "You might know your way around the forge, but you've a lot to learn about women."

A warm flush crept over my cheeks as I started up the stairs again. Tur slid passed to sit next to Gael, taking her hand casually. I wished I had that kind of ease around women.

"Evening, Gael, Emma," I said, proud I didn't stutter too badly. Emma's smile weakened my knees to the point of me sitting a bit harder than intended.

"Evening, Quinn. Tur mentioned you'd be comin' tonight," Emma said quietly. She reached down next to her leg and brought out a small tin bucket covered over with an off-white fabric. "I brought some biscuits to share. I know you work late at the forge and didn't think you'd have time to eat."

"That was nice of you," I said, trying not to stare. "We got off a bit early, but I didn't get to eat."

She pulled the fabric off, folding it with a quick efficiency I'd never be able to accomplish. I wondered if everything she did was magical. She handed me a biscuit, and I took a large bite.

"Delicious," I muttered, spraying crumbs on the row in front of us. An older man stood and turned to say something, but then thought better of it and sat down. I pulled out my water skin filled with beer. I offered it to Emma.

She accepted and took a swig of the ale.

"Thank you, Quinn."

She handed it back, and I took a swallow before putting the stopper back in.

It was fully dark now except for the gas lanterns that ringed the lower level. Mudstone lamps, which needed no flame, lit the upper level, in the Grand Pavilion, situated in the center of the seats, and where Lord Magus Usorin's family and invited guests sat. Grand artificer lamps, which were as bright as the sun without a flicker or smell to offend the powerful wizards of Bradenbridge, lit his private reception area. Each one cost more than I made in a year and were difficult to find. Most were passed down from parents to their children. I'd seen a broken lamp once that Ruari had repaired; the lamp would work forever unless you broke it like that one had been. It took an Artificer to fix the light, but we did all the other repairs.

The crowd hushed as Neff, the arena's owner, stepped to the center platform.

"Tonight, we have a display in magical prowess. Kyla, of House Acouver, has challenged Stirling, of House Ovro, to combat to settle a debt of honor. Combat ends when a combatant's shield fails."

The crowd booed as Neff strolled off, though he waved to the crowd as if they cheered his passage. Ushers turned down the lights as the magi climbed onto their platforms. A loud whirring noise filled the arena. They bowed to each other before the circular platforms rose fifteen feet in the air. The upper seats had a much better view, but we could see both magi to our left and right.

I took another bite of biscuit, glancing at Emma as she waited with her hands clenched in front of her. I returned my gaze to the fight momentarily, but rather preferred watching her.

Kyla struck first, thrusting her arm at her opponent, an arc of lightning shooting at her command. A blue haze formed before Stirling easily absorbed the shot. He returned a gout of flame that fell short of his intended target. Catcalls erupted from the crowd.

Tur laughed louder than anyone. "Guess he can't keep it up." Laughs from around us added to the raucous crowd.

Kyla threw three glowing orbs at Stirling, causing his shields to flicker dangerously. He cursed loudly as he returned fire with a swift flame strike that crashed into her shields; they flared green under the impact but held strong.

"I guess you should have been in your cups to duel me, Stirling," Kyla taunted. "Must be you need a great deal of wine before you face a woman who is too much for you to handle."

"Bitch," Stirling screamed, unleashing a barrage of fire-balls, some of which even hit her shield. The rest flared against the arena's defenses, and the audience shrieked as the impact lit up the invisible energy shield. His assault faltered then failed altogether, leaving the red-faced man panting from exertion.

"Ah, your power faded quickly, just like your wits."

Laughter and jabs assaulted Stirling, who screamed down at the crowds below him. "Shut up. Commoners are beneath my notice. You should respect your betters."

The crown responded with throwing curses and garbage at the mage in equal measure. A duel was one time commoners were allowed to ridicule the upper class.

Kyla sent a single shot of lightning toward the center of his shields, which flicked and went out, ending the match. Victorious, she dropped her shields, bowing to the crowd's cheers.

We leapt to our feet, shouting to the winner. Normally, I didn't enjoy the duels, but Stirling Ovro was a major ass and watching Kyla rake him over the coals had been amazing.

Without warning, Stirling produced a fireball and hurled it at Kyla's exposed back. It struck her solidly between the shoulder blades. The explosion threw the magus from her platform to land, sprawled out in the sand below, unmoving.

"Arrest him," Neff yelled as he entered the arena. "You know the rules of the arena, Stirling."

Seeing armed bruisers closing in on him, he leapt from his platform, rolling as he landed. He threw a blast of flame that lit the closest guard up like a bonfire. The man's agonized screams echoed through the arena.

Emma shrieked as the mage killed in front of us. I pushed her behind me, as if I'd be an effective shield against a fireball.

Two more bursts of flame and two more guards were engulfed in flame as Stirling headed toward the tunnel we'd come in. Before I knew it, I was moving, racing down the stairs to stop him. Stirling had broken the one rule of the duels and wasn't going to get away with it. As I reached the bottom, I dove for the fleeing wizard. I heard something snap as my weight drove into his side and I tackled him to the ground. We tumbled across the opening of the tunnel, my arms fastened around his waist. My head hit the wall hard; my arms went numb from the shock.

Stirling righted himself and stood over me.

"I'll teach a common piece of trash to touch their betters." He pointed his arm at me, and nothing happened. Shock spread across his face as his magic failed him once again.

Without another word, he ran out of the arena and into the night.

"You are a lucky cuss," Tur said as he held his hand out for me. I took it and he helped me to my feet. I rubbed the back of my head and winced at the bump there. Given I could be a pile of ash, I'd take the pain. What had I been thinking?

Emma stood on the bottom step, staring at me. "I'm not sure if that was the bravest or dumbest thing I've ever seen."

Gael grasped Emma's arm, affixing me with an icy glare.

"I'd say it was the dumbest. Get yourself killed for what? Glory? Maybe a couple coppers from Neff?" She turned to Emma. "Come on, we've got better things to do than spend time with stupid boys." With that, they left.

Tur scratched his head, a befuddled look on his face. "Well, you certainly messed up my evening plans, hero."

My head ached, and I'd almost died, but Emma thought I was brave...or stupid. I wasn't sure which it was, but I'd made an impression.

"Beers on you, Quinn," Tur said with a grin. "If I'm gonna have to look at your ugly face all night, I'm gonna need a bunch of ale."

I watched Emma's back as she exited the tunnel into the night.

"Yeah, I think I might need a few too."

So much for "the hero always gets the girl."

3

After a night at the Broken Spoke, morning came earlier than it should have. Tur had disappeared with some woman after an hour or so, but I'd made the mistake of staying on, talking with the hostlers and wainwrights, and drinking ale until my purse ran dry. My pounding head informed me that I'd made the wrong decision.

Master Smith Ruari provided a bunk room for any who wanted to stay or had nowhere else to go, like me. As usual, I was the only one there as I rose from my straw pallet and pulled on my boots. Regardless of my splitting headache, the forge required work before the day began.

The sun had barely crept into the sky as I entered the forge. I took to starting the coal fires and set out buckets for Alarik to fill when he got there. He still lived with his parents down a ways. It wouldn't be long 'fore they had him married off to some tradesman's daughter with a good dowry. My mom had died before I'd been old enough for such things. Master Ruari took me in, taught me the trade, and kept a roof over my head. Couldn't ask for much more.

I swung through the farrier forge and got it all going. Bran appeared as I set the last fire a burnin'.

"Mornin', Bran."

"Mornin'. I heard about you tryin' to stop the rogue wizard last night. Wish I'd been there, I'd have punched the shit out of him."

I didn't meet his eyes. "Well, kinda stupid on my part, and after all that, he got away."

"Quinn, you're lucky you ain't dead. I count that as a win, ole son." Bran hefted his hammer, bringing it down with a ringing blow on the anvil, my headache flaring with each strike. "I'd have smashed him good."

"Well, he got away, so that's that." I returned to the main forge. We had one more day to get the furnace and all the parts loaded and ready to move.

Ruari sat at the work bench in the back, tinkering with one of the valves from the steam-powered air blower. He handed me a small bucket like the one Emma had last night. "Wife says you don't eat enough. How's she gonna marry you off being all skin and bones."

I pulled off the cloth and dug into a half loaf of pumpkin bread. It was delicious. Ruari's wife, Miranda, had been sending down breakfast for me since I was seven with some variation of me not eating enough. It had become her ritual over the years.

"Thing about mechanical systems is they always want to break at the worst times." He held up the valve, turning it back and forth in his hands. "See that ridge?"

"Yes, sir."

"If I leave that ridge, moisture will collect and then it will rust over time. Might take years for it to fail, but better to fix it now and not have issues down the line. Course, I could leave it, probably be your problem to fix by then."

He smiled at me like my Ma used to.

"You'll outlive us all. I swear you're mostly metal and gears."

He laughed a deep, hearty laugh that could be heard across the yard.

"Maybe so. I need you and Tur to head up to the keep this morning to get the brackets installed. Usorin's gave us use of his newest golem. It'll lift the furnace into place right quick. Better than havin' to get twenty horses to lift that bastard. You should have figured that into the design, Quinn."

"Seems to me that you designed it." I grinned as we played out our old, familiar banter. "I'd have built it in parts and assembled it on site."

"Oh, yeah? How were you gonna get those welds hot enough at the keep to hold? Got a supply of wizards around to throw fire at it?"

I didn't answer, letting my grin do the talking. I knew I'd been maneuvered into a corner.

"Speaking of wizards. Heard about your heroics at the arena last night."

He fixed me with a stern eye as he spoke.

"You could have been killed, and fer what? That mage would spit in your face rather than look at ya. I don't care if she were pretty, but you don't go messin' with the magi. They're dangerous, Quinn."

I thought about explaining how I'd wanted to impress Emma, but Ruari was right. It'd been stupid and dangerous, and in the end, it hadn't impressed her an ingot's worth.

"I know. It won't happen again."

Ruari set down the valve and put his hand on my shoulder.

"You've got a good head on your shoulders. Don't let a pretty face cause you to lose it."

Heat flooded my face. "Tur's got a big mouth."

The big man laughed. "That he does, but it was Master

Haim told me about the dressin' down that pretty seamstress gave ya. She'll come 'round, just give it time."

I nodded, though I didn't believe what he said. A girl that pretty always had more than enough suitors.

"Well, I see Tur's here. Go on up to the keep and make sure his struts are in there good an' tight. That beast of yours is gonna weigh a ton full."

"I'll take care of it."

I left Ruari, stopped to fill my water bottle, and grabbed a straw hat before getting Tur. Tur looked about how I felt. Dark bags drooped under his red-shot eyes. He grimaced as he saw me approach.

"Aww, Quinn. I ain't got it in me to start hammerin' iron already."

"Good thing we're headed to the keep to double check your supports. Get the toolbox and let's go."

I'd have said Tur went off to get the tools, but I'd seen elderly women walking faster than he did. After a good ten minutes, he returned with the traveling toolbox and his water bottle. His head hung low as he stumbled across the forge in a pathetic attempt to get out of walking to the keep.

"I'll drag you by your hair if I need to. The struts are your handiwork, so you need to look them over."

I'd known Tur long enough to know that he'd do just about anything to get out of a day's work. I always thought it would be faster to just get it over with, but that was me.

He straightened up a bit as he approached.

"All right. Let's go."

We made good time crossing Bradenbridge, avoiding the carriages of the magi and the wagons of the haulers. I'd seen those drivers whip the commoners if they didn't move fast enough. If you wore the robes, you could stand in the middle of the street all day and not a word would be said about it, lest another wizard came along. They were a strange bunch. Messing with magic must change a soul.

I noticed more people than normal moving quickly toward the center of town, the younger ones running. I grabbed the arm of a dirty beggar boy, who slapped at my hand, his eyes wild.

"Calm it," I snapped at him and he settled. "What's all the fuss about?"

He grinned like an ol' tabby cat. "Watch Guard caught Stirling. Gonna fry the bastard in the square."

I loosed him and he bolted off into the flow of people.

"Looks like we need to break for some entertainment," Tur said as he followed the crowd toward the town square. "Those Watch are some tough bastards."

I nodded my agreement as I followed along. It had been years since a member of the Watch had been sighted in Bradenbridge. News of Stirling's attack on his rival Magus must have spread fast to bring them here. The crowd thickened as we entered the square.

Stirling stood on a raised platform, his outstretched arms and legs tied to the wooden X positioned at the back. His face looked beaten, from what I could see. His robes were torn, hanging around him like scraps at the tanner's shop.

A man in black robes with silver symbols around his cuffs and hem stood next to Usorin. The Lord Magus of Bradenbridge spoke, his hands gesturing as he did so. As one of the liege lords of Astaria, he protected the vassal families, though no one could stop the Watch when the law had been broken. The man in black shook his head once. Usorin's face turned red as he continued speaking to the Watch guard. He grabbed the guard's arm and pulled him to face him.

Faster than I thought possible, the Watch guard slammed a fist into Usorin's gut, knocking him back. A collective gasp rose from the crowd, who then went silent. The Watch were

Arch Magus Everard's personal enforcers and the only ones that could discipline a magus.

The guard turned to face the crowd.

"The Watch has condemned Stirling Abel to death for his unlawful assault on Kyra Nilsen."

Stirling screamed as the guard turned to face him. He pleaded for his life, calling for Usorin to save him. The Lord Magus had regained his feet and stood staring the Watch guard as Stirling railed against the injustice of his situation.

"You have been found unworthy of your station, Stirling Abel. Death is your punishment."

The guard's arm came up slowly and Stirling's wailing increased with it. When the guard's arm pointed directly at the fallen magus, a burst of flame belched forth and consumed the screaming man.

The smell of burning meat filled the air as Stirling paid for his attack on Kyra. I could hear vomiting around me and noticed that one of the affected was Tur.

Justice had a steep price in Bradenbridge that day.

4

The day to fire the Usorin's furnace had come at last. I followed Ruari through the morning haze as we made our way to the manor to test the new furnace system. The smells of wood burning in hearths around Bradenbridge scented the air as we climbed the hill that led up to Usorin's keep. The stocky, stone structure covered the top of the broad hill, whence was given a good view of Bradenbridge and the surrounding countryside. A large staircase led into the keep, but we veered around the building and down a slope to where the furnace had been assembled the previous day.

Workers carried bags of coal and loaded the massive forge that stood on a series of stout metal supports to allow air intake from the bottom. The assembly that Ruari built stood at the front and was connected to the main air channel that Usorin's carpenters had installed in the spring. Bran and Tur went to inspect the understructure for any signs of weakness or damage from the install, while I followed Ruari as he climbed to the top of the furnace. It contained a series of doors for coal to be deposited in for burning, but only the forward section had coal for testing. Once the fire burned, the heat would generate steam from the boiling chamber, which drove the gears to push the hot air through the channel into the keep. We'd built two smaller systems to ensure it would work.

A commotion sounded below us as Usorin led three red-robed magi toward the furnace.

"Ruari," he yelled as he approached. "Why is this not running yet?"

Ruari sighed deeply.

"Allow me to come down, my Lord, to speak with you."

We returned to the base of the furnace where a red-faced Usorin waited on us.

"Good mornin', my Lord."

"What is good about it?" He pointed at the furnace. "Why is there not warm air flowing through my keep? The blasted thing is set up. Make it work."

People trickled out of the keep, excited to see the new furnace operating. An audience was just what we needed. Failure in front of Usorin would be bad; add a laughing audience and the Lord Magus might have a fit.

"We are preparin' now, my Lord." Ruari gestured to the line of men carrying coal up to the furnace. "They are loadin' the front chamber so we can test the workin's. If all goes well, you'll have heat tomorrow."

"Tomorrow?" Usorin asked, his face going redder by the moment. "Tomorrow is unacceptable." He looked around until he saw Cameron, the head of the laborers. "Cameron, come here."

Cameron, a stocky man with a large pot belly, stomped over to Usorin, bowing his head in respect.

"Me, Lord?"

"The furnace must be filled to full by noon."

"Noon, Sire?" Cameron blanched at the thought of

porting hundreds of pounds of coal up a hill to fill the huge burner.

"Yes, noon. I don't care what you have to do, but if you fail me, I will be very unhappy."

"Yes, my Lord. I'll gather every hand."

Ruari cleared his throat. "If I may, Sire, the furnace will take about a day to get to temperature."

"I will take care of the fire, Master Smith." Usorin smirked. "I expect everything to be running by this evening."

He turned and stalked back to the keep. We watched him go.

Ruari spoke up. "Cam, you can use my boys to help. That'll give you three more pairs of hands."

Cameron swallowed hard.

"Thanks. No way we'll be done in time."

"If you can get a layer across the bottom, we'll have enough to run the thing," I said, thinking of how to help. "Set your men up fire-line style and pass the bags. It will save us from walking and speed it up. Master, if you set a winch, we can hook up the lift and pull the coal up to the top."

"Good idea, Quinn." He turned to Cameron. "Send a runner to town and get everyone you can. I don't want to face his Lordship if this doesn't work."

Cameron nodded and left, calling to his men and explaining the plan. A boy ran off at a good clip down the hill to Bradenbridge.

The magus would be the end of us the way things were going.

As the sun reached its peak, Usorin and his flock of red-robed magi emerged from the keep. We'd finished loading the coal earlier than expected, so we lit the fires and sat back to wait. People from the keep and the town had gathered to see the remarkable contraption work. People sat on the grass or wandered around the furnace marveling at the size of the thing.

Ruari motioned me to my feet as the Lord Magus approached. We both went to one knee as he joined us, his three lackeys standing behind him.

"Master Smith, are we ready to begin?" he asked impatiently. "I would see your machine working now."

We stood.

"Master, we've lit the fires. We should have enough heat to start the test in a few hours."

Usorin flicked his hand dismissively.

"I have ways at my disposal to generate heat more rapidly."

"I don't understand, my Lord," Ruari said slowly. "In a few hours, the coals will produce enough heat to run the boiler."

"Crimshaw," Usorin said over his shoulder. "Take the others to the top of the furnace and do as I told you."

"Yes, my Lord," Crimshaw's shaky voice answered. Each of the magi held a leather bag like it was a snake. Crimshaw walked slowly across the ramp up to the top of the furnace.

"Have your men open the hatches, and they will drop alarium on the coals and ignite it. You'll have enough heat to warm the keep in a few minutes. I'll be the envy of every Lord in Terralon."

"Alarium." Ruari's voice rose in surprise. "My Lord, how much is in each bag?"

Usorin scoffed.

"You worry like a mother hen, Master Smith. Each bag holds a rock the size of a man's fist or so. It will fuel the system for months."

If each rock weighed a half-pound, there would be enough there to level a town, if it was refined. If not, the explosion could destroy the keep and kill everyone in it depending on the ore content.

Panic edged into Ruari's voice.

"That much refined alarium would level the hill we're on, Sire. Please, don't use the alarium."

"Ruari, you are vexing me," Usorin said, eyes narrowed as he glared at the smith. "Do you think me stupid? Those rocks barely contain enough alarium to burn, let alone explode."

"I don't think you're stupid, Sire," Ruari said quickly. "The furnace wasn't built to hold the heat that alarium produces. It could crack the iron or melt holes in it."

Usorin pushed past Ruari. The wizards stood apart, one at each opening. The heat distorted the air between us, making them look more like ghosts than men. "Drop the bags and ignite them," the Lord Magus commanded from below.

"No!" Ruari screamed from behind Usorin. "You'll kill us all!"

Flame burst from the hands of each of the wizards as they followed their orders. The loud crash of the hatches closing announced they had completed their task. A loud whirring noise emanated from the blower at the head of the furnace as it came to life.

Usorin whirled on Ruari, his eyes flashing with anger.

"How dare you countermand me in front of my people? I'll have you strung up for such insolence."

Ruari bowed his head. "My Lord, my only thought is for your safety. Please, do what you will to me, but you need to flee. I fear the worst is about to happen."

"You are such an ignorant peasant, Ruari. This is why—"

If the wizard said anything more, it was lost in the confusion as all hell broke loose. A cracking noise filled the area as the boiling chamber collapsed. Screams of pain followed as scalding water burst in all directions, covering the nearest people. The cries turned to shrieks of panic as the dull black metal began to glow a fierce red.

"What have you done?" Ruari said over the noise. "You've killed us all."

"Me? This is your machine and you are to blame!" Usorin screamed over the wails of agony and fear as people fled the site. The sides of the furnace pulsed with barely contained heat. Usorin pulled his sword, the blade instantly igniting with the stored alarium fire. "You'll pay for your insolence!"

Without thinking, I stepped in front of my master, arms held out wide to protect him. The sword swung down directly at my head.

"Ruari, run!"

The furnace bucked as the super-heated metal began to deform. The ground shook and the sword missed my head. Over-balanced from the swing, Usorin fell face-first, catching himself on his hands before impact. I looked down and saw a severed arm laying on the ground. No time to worry about that; I had to get Ruari away from there.

Ruari stumbled down the hill as the ground continued to shake. Fear drove my steps, knowing we would die if we stopped. I faltered as the ground heaved again. I fought to regain my balance but lost control completely when my foot snagged on a body and I pitched forward. It saved my life by getting me away from the unfolding scene.

I rolled head over tail down the sharp incline as the furnace spewed fire like a dragon from the legends. It wasn't until I stopped at the bottom in a copse of trees that I noticed something was wrong. It took me a bit to clear my head before I realized what had happened. My right arm was missing from just below the shoulder. The wound had been burned shut by the flame blade. The seal had saved my life, but my blacksmithing career was destroyed.

I cried until the darkness took me.

5

The sound of clomping hooves was the first thing I became aware of. I could smell horse and oats as I fought my way out of unconsciousness. It was dark around me, but the gentle sway and occasional bounce let me know I rode in a wagon. Pain flared in my right arm as I tried to move it. I groaned as the memory hit me that my right arm was gone.

"Ah, so you aren't dead." A voice came from over my head. The canvas that covered me moved to show a black-hooded figure with glowing silver symbols around the cuffs of his robe; the Watch guard. Panic must have shown on my face as he said, "Hang on there, I mean you no harm."

"What happened?" I croaked out through impossibly dry lips. My mouth cracked in multiple places, rewarding me with the taste of blood. The man lowered his hood, and I felt the wagon move as he climbed in next to me. He held my head up and gave me a bit of water.

"Not sure what happened. There were dead bodies all over the hillside when I arrived to talk to Usorin." He gave me another sip of water. "I found you out cold at the bottom of the hill. From the way you're dressed, I'm guessing a blacksmith."

I nodded slowly, eying the water skin.

"You don't want to drink too fast or you'll vomit." He gave me another short drink, then sat back. "Thought you could use some help, and I have need of a blacksmith."

"What good is a one-armed smith?" I forced out through clenched teeth. The scene played back as I saw the blade descend. I'd been so fixated on protecting Ruari that I hadn't noticed the blade slicing through my arm. Flame blades held a razor-sharp edge, and the fire closed the wound as fast as they sliced flesh open. No wonder Usorin loved it so much. He could maim his victim and they'd live through it.

"Right now, not much," the guard said. He reached up and pulled back his hood, exposing a head of gray hair. He had bug-eyes and a sculpted metal plate where his mouth should be. I tried to move away from him, but I was too weak.

"Sorry about that, lad," he said as he reached up and removed his face. "I forgot I had the mask on."

He removed the mask, revealing an older man with a thin, pointed nose and wrinkles around vivid blue eyes.

"I'll explain more once we get home, but you're safe. I'm going to put you under the tarp so you can get some sleep."

After one more sip of water, he returned to the wagon's seat and pulled the tarp over me, cutting off the sunlight. I wondered what to make of all this, but I knew one thing for certain: my life would never be the same again.

The sun was going down when the tarp was removed. I saw trees all around me and knew we were far from

Bradenbridge. The wagon pulled into a small barn. I pulled myself to a seated position as the Watch guard unhitched the horses and stabled them, speaking in low, soothing tones. The barn had four stalls, but I only saw the two horses. The main section of the barn held hay bales and a tack board. A cloth tarp covered what looked like a boat. Why have a boat when there was no water for days in any direction?

Once he finished, the old man came to help me to my feet.

"You're a big one."

He positioned himself under my good arm as I slid down from the wagon.

"Why do you have a boat in the middle of the forest?" I asked as we passed the covered item.

"Ahh, just me trying to be a bird. Nothing to worry about."

I started to ask more, but I stumbled as he helped me out of the barn. He grunted as he helped me across the yard to a small, ramshackle shack in the middle of the forest. A giant tree loomed over the house, making it look like a child's toy. Three chickens pecked away under an oak tree.

We stumbled across the uneven ground to the front door of his home. The door swung in on loud, creaky hinges. The inside was bare except for a table, two chairs, and a wash basin. A door led into the back of the building.

A wooden handrail ran around the middle of the small room. With a grunt, he leaned me against the left wall.

"Hold on to the rail with your good hand. There will be a jerk as we start."

He went to the back door. This one swung open silently, revealing a metal box open toward us.

"I know it don't look like much but can't tell a nut by its shell." He chuckled at his own joke as he pulled down a metal grate in front of him. I held on to the railing, but almost toppled when the floor lurched. It felt like we were moving, but without windows, it was hard to tell. The room swayed and banged as it rose, and I tightened my grip, though I didn't know what good it would do. I swayed as the thing came to a stop. The man pushed the gate up and helped me into his home.

As we stepped into the foyer, I gasped. In front of me stood a massive copper cylinder with all sorts of odd pieces attached to it; a boiler, from the looks of it, to produce steam.

The rest of the room was a small, neatly decorated sitting area. He helped me over to one of the overstuffed leather chairs and lowered me into it; my mouth hung open the whole time.

He took a seat in my chair's twin. "Ah, that's better." The man said with a sigh.

The rest of the room screamed of the man's wealth. Alarium lamps were affixed to the walls on either side of large glass windows, revealing a view of the canopy of trees that surrounded the place. I'd never earn enough in my lifetime to buy one panel of that window. I looked at him and asked, "Who are you?"

He stood, straightened his robe, and bowed to me.

"I am Roland, the Chief Artificer for the Arch Magus of Astaria, at your service."

"Arch Magus? You mean the ruler of Astaria?"

"That would be the one," he said with a chuckle. "I am also a member of the Watch, charged with enforcing the laws of the land on the magi who live within our borders."

"Why did you help me, err, my Lord?" I must have hit my head harder than I thought to speak so to a Watch guard.

"No 'my lords' or 'Sire' or that bullshit. You call me Roland and I'll call you..."

I waited for him to tell me what he would call me, but realized he wanted my name.

"Oh, Quinn."

"Quinn it is." He pulled a stool over and dropped himself onto it. "So, tell me what happened, 'cause when I got there, it looked like hell had broken loose."

I thought for a moment, trying to piece together the events of the day. I started by telling him about building the furnace and how the master smith had built a device to push the air to the keep.

Roland interrupted me. "Would that be Master Ruari?"

"Yes, sir." That earned me a stern look. "Sorry, Roland."

"Better. I've had some dealings with Ruari over the years. You must be the orphan boy he took in. You were probably about ten when I saw you last."

I stifled tears as I said, "I think he's dead." For the second time in my life I was an orphan. I'd lost the only father I'd ever known.

Roland nodded and indicated for me to continue. I told the story in as much detail as I could remember, and he stopped me to ask questions before I got to the part where Usorin cut my arm off.

"Will you burn him like Stirling for what he did to me?" I asked.

A puzzled expression came over Roland's face.

"Why would I do that?"

I pushed down an anger I hadn't even known I held.

"He tried to kill Master Ruari and sliced my arm clean off. Doesn't that deserve punishment?"

"Not from the Watch. We only step in if you harm or kill another noble. The magi can do whatever they want to their subjects, as long as they leave the other noble families alone. He'll pay those families if the magus that he sent to stoke the flames died, which sounds likely."

"That's not right. He killed all those people. Is there no justice for the dead?"

"Quinn, the world we live in is unfair to be certain, but we'll discuss this later."

"When can I go back to the smithy? Ruari will be worried about me and he'll need help training up my replacement. I can probably still help around the shop, even missing an arm."

Roland didn't look at me as he answered. "Son, they all think you're dead and you might as well be. Ruari's a good man, but he couldn't keep a one-armed man around. I brought you here to save you the pain of bein' cast out. Do ya understand?"

I nodded. "My life really is over." Pain flooded through me as I realized, my adopted family thought me dead. I'd never get to see any of them again. Never drink with Tur or teach Alarik new techniques of forging. "I'm sorry you wasted the effort in saving me. You should have just let me die."

Roland watched me for a long moment. "Our first order of business is to get you on your feet and healthy." He looked around the room. "Jabber, where are you?"

A lanky man stepped into the room from the far entryway. His metal skin was a burnished copper color, and he wore a stubby mustache over his thin lips. As he got close, I could see he had strange eyes and bolts fastening him together.

"How do you have a metal golem?" I asked. "Only the most powerful magi can summon them."

Roland laughed. "I see I've got my work cut out for me. This is Jabber, my automaton butler."

"Automaton? He's a golem. Why would you call him such? Are you a mage?"

"I'll answer all your questions in good time. Jabber here's gonna help you get healthy and ready for the second step."

"Second step?"

"I'd thought it'd be obvious. We're going to build you a new arm."

I had no idea what to say to that.

6

Over the next few months, Jabber became my constant companion while Roland traveled on Watch business. He brought me food, helped me get dressed, and worked to help me regain my balance. My missing arm ached all the time; I'd reach for things with it, having forgotten for a moment that it was gone. I cried like a babe or raged at the injustice of it all. Over time, the loss was no less profound, but I adapted to having only one arm.

I'd been confined to the main part of the lab since my arrival. I had a bedroom to myself, a bathroom with running water, and an indoor privy that took all the waste away. As nice as it was, I'd have given anything to return to the straw mat and Ruari's forge. Jabber gave me the tour, pointing out the kitchen, small workshop, and Roland's living quarters.

I'd passed the same locked door every day. The first time I saw Jabber pass through the door I asked what was in there.

"Master Quinn, that is the Artificer's workshop. Master Roland left word that you are to be restricted from entering until he deems fit."

"Deems fit?" What the hell did that mean? "What do I have to do to be allowed access?"

Jabber cocked his head at the question.

"I'm sure I don't know, but I would conjecture that you must be more than you are now."

The perfect non-answer. Jabber could be good company, but rarely gave useful information about Roland or the Treetop Workshop.

Roland showed up with food and provisions, and occasionally we would talk about blacksmithing and working with metals.

Jabber and I spent evenings with him teaching me to read. I'd seen letters and knew some numbers from working in the forge, but Ruari's wife kept the books and sales records, so I'd never learned. I hated it. I was already useless as a one-armed blacksmith; what difference did it make if I could read?

Roland insisted, and Jabber followed his orders, so I learned—slowly at first, but then, once I stopped fighting it, at a better pace. By the end of four months, I could read most of the words in any book that Jabber handed me and could do sums and naughts, and some rough math they called trigonometry.

One day, Roland arrived still wearing his Watch robes. Something about him was different. He unlocked the door to the artificer's workshop and bade me follow him. I did as told, and when he turned up the lights, I gaped in wonder. At the far end of the room stood a forge with an anvil. The rest of the room held an assortment of devices that I'd never seen, but they all looked amazingly complex. He pointed to a stool on one side of the workbench, and he took a seat on the other side.

"Jabber tells me you're doing well with your studies and you are adapting well to the loss of your arm. What do you think, lad?" he asked, his tone more serious than I'd ever heard.

"If that's what he says, then I'd take him at his word."

I wasn't sure what was going on, but I shifted uneasily on the stool like I'd been caught doing something wrong.

Roland gave me a sly look. "That's not what I asked, is it?"

"No, sir. I'm good. I feel stronger and my stump doesn't hurt as often. I think it's time for me to leave."

Roland passed over the "sir" comment, a sure sign that he wasn't himself today. "And where would you go?"

I shook my head resigned to what the fates had chosen for me. "I'll head south. Since I can't go back to my old life, I figure I'll try to make a life as a scribe. I can read now and my handwriting is passable."

"After being a smith, you think a scribe will suit ya?"

I shrugged. "With one arm, I don't have many options. It would have been kinder to let me die."

"Nah, I'm not one to throw out a valuable asset, just because of some surface damage."

I held out my stump. "Does this look like surface damage to you? My life is over, its time I face the facts."

Roland considered me for a long while. "As you know, I am a member of the Watch. Our sworn duty is to enforce the laws that the Arch Magus sets down, but we have another purpose as well."

He held up his hand and flames burst forth, as I'd seen him do when he executed Stirling. Standing, he removed his robes and I couldn't believe my eyes. A series of tubes ran from a gauntlet around his forearm to a tank strapped to his hip. Another device was attached to a bracer that ran from the wrist to the elbow of his left arm. Copper cylinders ran the length of his forearm, attached to the metal bracer with a series of fasteners.

"What is all this?" I asked, stunned by the display. "I thought you were a wizard, like Usorin."

He sat back down. "Well, that's the first part of the story. For the most part, there is no magic."

I didn't say a word for a long while. No magic? I'd watched wizards duel my whole life, lived in fear of them, bowed before them. Was I to now understand they were all fakes?

"Alarium," I said, as the facts clicked in my head. That was the reason for all the secrecy around Usorin's flame blade. "The magi use alarium to power the devices so that it looks like magic."

Roland grinned at me. "I knew you'd be a quick study, but you surprise me, lad. Most take a lot longer to come to grips with it."

"That explains so much. Ruari said the magi filled the alarium with magic."

"Not quite. Alarium contains an energy most refer to as magic, but it's not. Usorin is powerful because his land contains one of the few alarium mines in all of Astaria. He regulates how much the other Magi families receive. He basically controls the source of magic in the land," Roland explained patiently.

I thought about it before asking my next question.

"You said *the* source of magic, but there must be more, or he'd keep it all and become the Arch Magus. What am I missing?"

Roland's smile grew. "The Watch creates the devices that transform the alarium into the magic the magi display. If Usorin gets greedy or stubborn, his rivals will simply get better devices and he falls behind."

I thought back to the arena and the duel. "That's why Kyra defeated Stirling so easily. His flames couldn't penetrate her shields."

Roland agreed. "The shield generator uses the alarium to create a barrier. The Ovro family only has flame devices so Kyra chose shields to protect against it. Stronger families have wider choices of weapons and shields. The Arch Magus tells us which families to give the devices too. It keeps the balance of power and avoids a civil war."

"But she didn't expect him to fire on her after he lost."

"No, she didn't. Stirling was an arrogant ass and got what he deserved. His family irritated powerful people and their access had been curtailed. In a futile attempt to regain his family's standing, he was trying to marry Kyra and took it a bit too far when she said no. Astaria is better off without him." Roland cleared his throat before continuing. "Part of being with the Watch involves creating new devices and improving on the ones we have. We never release the best of anything to the wizards. The Watch can never lose."

"Then why me? I can't create anything with one arm."

"Quinn, you were a great smith and will be a better artificer. As you saw with Stirling, being part of the Watch means killing when necessary. I'd like you to become a member of the Watch, but you have to be able to carry out all the duties, not just build things. Can you do that? Do you even want to?"

I hadn't thought of that. Roland had saved my life. With Jabber's help, he'd nursed me back to health, taught me to read, and more. My adopted family thought me dead and Roland was as close as I'd ever have to another one, but still it bothered me. "So we kill anyone the Arch Magus doesn't like?"

He shook his head. "Our charter is to maintain the balance, limit alarium technology, and protect Astaria from outside forces. In order to accomplish these goals, we will kill, steal, and anything else necessary."

"It sounds like we're the bad guys," I said simply.

Roland chuckled. "I suppose it does at that, but Quinn,

people like Stirling don't stop at anything. Before the Watch, Magi ran amok, committing atrocities on a massive scale. Fights between families would lay waste regions worth of land and people."

I hadn't learned about such things at the smithy nor in the books I'd read, though most of those were on metallurgy, not politics and history. "How did it all stop?"

"As the magic grew weaker, Everard forced the great families into an alliance to fight the Norns. They attempted to invade, but Everard's magic turned the tide and sunk the Norn fleet in the process. The threat of Astaria's magic keeps the other nations from attacking us. If a greedy family sold our technology to the enemy, they could wipe out our whole nation."

"If I join the Watch, I'll be required to do those things as well?" I didn't like the sounds of them, but Roland had been so good to me and it was a way I could protect Ruari and the others, even if they thought me dead. Joining the Watch would make me useful again.

"Yes, and more, but you'll be protecting Astaria in the process."

The draw of having a purpose pulled me toward the decision I knew I'd already made. "I'll join."

An hour later, Roland swore me in as an official member of the Watch. "You'll meet Everard soon enough, but we've got other concerns. Well, we're at step two," Roland said with a grin.

"Step two?"

"Step one was getting you healthy and educated. Step two was building you an improved arm." He stood and went to a cabinet near the forge. He pulled out a large object covered in cloth and returned to his stool. He laid the package on the table between us, as if presenting a new baby to its parent. "Open it."

My fingers trembled as I reached out and pulled the cloth aside. A brass and steel arm emerged from the wrappings. A series of straps hung from the shoulder rigging.

"It's beautiful. How does it work?"

Roland rounded the table, taking a copper piece out of the opening to the arm. He fitted it around my stump, securing the sliding pieces with small screws until the fit was snug, but not tight. He slid it off and attached it to the arm after connecting a series of tubes. After pushing the arm into place and buckling the leather harness around my shoulders, he adjusted the straps and fiddled with the controls.

"Try her out."

I flexed my fingers, but nothing happened. I tried to lift my arm, but it hung lifeless, just a piece of metal dangling from my shoulder. Roland huffed, taking a tool from the pouch on his belt. He mumbled to himself as he adjusted the arm.

"Try now."

I willed the fingers to curl and after a moment they did. I flexed them and they responded after a short delay.

"This is amazing."

Roland returned to his seat. "It takes time for the arm to integrate with your nervous system. In a few days it will function much like your natural arm."

I fought back tears as I watched the hand rise before my face. The motion wasn't smooth, but I could feel my arm again. After a few more movements the arm locked up.

"What happened?"

"There was only enough alarium to power it for a few minutes," Roland said as he drummed his fingers on the workbench. "I guess, we'll have to get it fitted with a full charge, don't ya think?"

My eyes welled with tears as I felt whole for the first time since the accident. I owed Roland everything. He'd saved my life, replaced my arm, and given me a purpose to live again when I thought all was lost.

"Yeah, that sounds good."

And it did.

7

Over the next few months, Roland didn't leave other than for provisions. I had full run of the Treetop Workshop, as he called it. Days were spent training for my new life as part of the Watch. I learned everything from combat to ballroom dance. Roland explained that we never knew when we'd need to mix in with the upper crust to get the information we needed.

In the evenings, we discussed metallurgic theory, alarium burn rates, transfer mechanics, and anything else that would aid in my being able to assemble new devices and weapons. Other times we reviewed the Norns and the other nations. We discussed trade, politics, and military capabilities. We spent the most time discussing the Norns, who had raided the Astaria coast until Everard had destroyed most of their navy. They'd sought to destroy Astaria ever since.

The workshop was a marvel. Roland taught me to work on each piece, how to fix it, and the component parts and theory behind the devices. Roland beamed with pride as he showed off the alarium core he'd developed. Made from an alloy I'd never heard of, it stored enough raw alarium to generate the workshop for the next hundred years. The core was the only piece he didn't teach me everything about. I learned to regulate it and the safety controls, but he kept the theories behind it to himself.

When I wasn't training, I spent my time building a new arm to use on missions for the Watch. I still wore the original arm that Roland had given me. It now worked as well as my old arm, though it didn't tire after hours of moving metal. My new obsession was upgrading my combat arm to give me an edge. I created a new forearm section first that was fitted with an electrical discharge adapter to throw electrical arcs. After seeing Kyra's display, I thought it would be practical and easy to use. After it was installed, Roland called for a field test of my new creation. Jabber assisted in fitting it to my mechanical arm, replacing the original portion. It took over an hour—with Jabber's help—to get the new piece attached. After that I determined I needed a way to inter-change these pieces without needing assistance. It would make it easier for me and I could swap out arm pieces in case of trouble.

The most visible part of the secret society was the control they maintained over the magi. What wasn't known was the number of missions involving espionage, assassination, and the theft of unsanctioned technological devices. Turns out, Ruari's policy of only building domestic machinery was a good one; other families who sought to loosen the grip of the Watch and create rival technology were squashed with ruth-less efficiency.

I met Roland in back of the barn downstairs. Trees provided cover from the sun and prying eyes, as airships were replacing coaches for long distant travel. The giant diri-gibles floated to all the cities of Astaria. Bradenbridge had recently built an airship tower of its own so flights could arrive from the capital. Roland turned to me as I approached.

"Lad, let's see what your new toy can do." He pointed to the metal cans that hung from ropes tied to the lower branches of the trees. "Six targets. Can you break them in that many shots?"

"Let's see."

I stepped to the line he'd scratched in the dirt. I pointed at the first can and fired. The electricity arced across the intervening space and missed, by a lot. A sapling burst into flames as the energy struck it. I ignored the hearty laugh from behind me, adjusting the flow output controls. The second shot missed by a lot less. Another adjustment and the can shattered, as did the second and third.

"Nice, but I count five shots and only three targets down. If those were men seeking your blood, you'd be done for."

I flipped over the optical lens that focused the energy into a single arc and pointed at the center target, leaving a can on either side. I fired. Instead of the single bolt piercing the one can, a wave of energy sprayed out, hitting all three and destroying them.

"I changed out the optics for a Phase inverter. It'll give you a spray pattern instead of a single bolt."

Roland's mouth hung open.

"Well, I'll be damned. I've never thought to use it in that application before."

"It's a heavy drain on the supply with one shot, but in a time of need, it's worth the risk." I secured the device, not wanting it to go off at an inopportune moment, like while I was relieving myself, 'cause that would be messy and painful. Just because I wore the device didn't mean I was insulated from its affects.

We discussed more applications for the optic lens and other ideas I'd had around the designs I'd been working on. Roland pointed out possible issues as well as other ways to look at problems. We took the lift to Treetop, both starving and ready to eat. Jabber had the table set and food on the table. I swore the automaton was psychic.

A sheet of parchment sat next to Roland's dinner. He read it over as we sat.

"Looks like we've got your first mission, lad."

Oh, boy.

I was in Ovrodon a week later, the second largest city in Terralon. The Ovro family still controlled the city named for them and were very proud of that fact—so proud, according to Roland's parchment, that they'd been buying parts to construct their own war automaton; the eldest son, Walden, had bragged about it at a state dinner. Now it was my job to get the plans and destroy any machinery I found.

Roland and I waited in a safe house a mile from the workshop where the informant said the automaton was being built. Once the moon was down, I went to work dressed all in black with mask in place, doing double duty protecting my identity and augmenting my abilities. I'd also created special gloves to go over my hands to protect them from the devices I wore. I headed down the darkened streets toward my target. I'd have liked more firepower, but without a robe to hide the extra pieces, I risked revealing secrets.

I made good time moving from shadow to shadow as Roland had taught me. Sweat trickled down my back as I went, the summer heat still lingering through the night. Circling the building told me little, since there were no windows; I was sure the Ovros didn't want anyone snooping around their secret projects.

I ducked behind the nearest building to examine the entrance. A single guard sat on a wooden stool, asleep. I moved in and hit him with the short, wooden bully I carried.

He grunted as the club hit. I caught him as he slumped, pushing him back on the stool, his head leaning against the wall as if he was still slept. I fished through his pockets and retrieved the key to the door.

Given the late hour, no one moved on the street. I slid the key into the lock and turned, hearing a distinct click. No sounds came from inside as I listened. The only thing I heard was the labored breathing of the unconscious guard. I cracked the door, waiting for an alarm or a cry from inside the building. When none came, I stepped inside, closing the door with a soft bump.

The goggles in my mask compensated for the lack of light, plunging the room in a greenish glow. It was enough to avoid running into the work benches, but smaller objects were blurred.

I found a bullseye lantern near the door and opened the shutter. A beam of light penetrated the darkness. The workshop was a single, large room, longer by far than it was wide. Cluttered work benches ran in rows, heading toward the fabrication shop at the opposite end. The coal forges still glowed in the distance. Either the smiths worked very late or, more likely, stoked the forge so it wasn't cold in the morning.

I crept along, holding the light below the top of the tall workspaces. I doubted anyone would be present at this hour, but I didn't want to draw any attention if they were. As I reached the end of the workspace, I paused to examine the fabrication area. Beside the forge, metal benders, steam pumps, and the like lined the walls. In the center of the space stood what I'd come for: the war automaton. Roughly human in shape, it stood at least seven feet tall. One arm ended in a nasty-looking saw blade; the other, a massive cleaver.

I'd brought three alarium bombs. All together, they would level the building after the timer ended. I took the first one out, ready to pull the stopper and start the countdown. This one would go near the forge.

Suddenly, lights flooded the workshop as a man stepped from behind the massive machine. He wore brilliant green robes, his long, blond hair pulled back in a tail behind his neck. He glared at me as he spoke.

"I wondered how long it would take the Watch to come see my new toy."

I straightened, setting the lantern on the floor. I doubted he was here to discuss schematics.

"Walden Ovro. The Watch requires the destruction of your machine. Stand aside and you won't be harmed."

My voice boomed through the space, amplified by the mask.

"Dramatic, aren't we?" He sneered at me. "The magi are restless and ready to throw off Arch Magus's yoke. Everard's reign is ending, and we will be free of him and his murdering Watch. I set a trap to lure you here and I'll be the first magus to kill one of you."

"I don't care about politics. I'm here to destroy your automaton. Stand aside."

I strode forward, appearing far braver than I felt.

Walden laughed.

"You might not want to come closer, assassin."

His tone stopped me cold.

"And why is that?"

He smiled at me.

"Because my war automaton is fully functional."

A whirring noise started as red eyes gleamed from the head of the war machine. It lurched forward, raising the saw as it spun up to full speed.

Being cut into kindling didn't suit me. I needed to think fast.

8

The automaton's heavy footfalls boomed as it closed in on me. I fired a burst of electricity at the machine, but it did nothing to slow its advance.

"Did you think I'd leave such an obvious weakness as to allow electricity to slow my creation?" Walden asked as he watched his machine close in with its spinning saw blade. If I didn't think of something quick, I'd be missing more than an arm. I backed up until I was between two work benches. As the automaton moved between them, I half jumped, half rolled over the nearest one, scattering an assortment of parts and tools as I went.

"You need not make such a mess," Walden remarked from his vantage point. "I'm going to have to have someone clean up after you."

"The only thing they'll be cleaning up is your blood," I said, cursing my bad luck. I snapped off a bolt of electricity in his direction and received a satisfying shriek as it struck near him. At least that would shut his mouth for a few. Stirling must have lost the families "magic" devices, since Walden wasn't firing at me.

The metal golem swung the blade across the bench towards me, forcing me to duck. The blade sent a shower of sparks from the edge of the bench as the metals ground against each other. Luckily, the benches were bolted to the floor or I'd be dodging them as well as the blades.

I fired another shot at the automaton's eyes, hoping to blind it, but that did as much as the first shot had. The cleaver crashed down next to me as I moved away from the mechanical death dealer. My left arm wore a gauntlet that fired small darts, which ignited as they flew. I fired a series of them at the optics again and one stuck, cracking the lens.

"I would think one machine should be easy against the might of the Watch." He sighed loudly. "I am so disappointed in you. I thought you'd have some amazing device that would shut down my golem in seconds. Don't tell me you didn't expect it to be resistant to fire and electricity?"

The slashing arm of the automaton's spinning blade prevented me from answering as I dove below it, keeping a bench between the giant and myself. It swung the saw blade at me time and again; though it couldn't get a clear hit on me, it did send the contents of the benches flying in all directions.

Walden's voice came from across the workshop.

"Seriously, my time is precious to me. Please hurry it up and let him kill you so I can get to sleep. I have an early breakfast with the Lord Magus."

The alarium lights were bright and offered no shadows to hide me. The far end stood in darkness except for the glowing coals of the forges. I caught glimpses of the wizard moving around to stay out of lightning range.

"I thought you were trying to overthrow Everard," I yelled over the machine's noise and crashing saw blade. "Why not stick a knife in Usorin? I guess you are too much the coward to do your own dirty work."

"The Watch has no idea what is going on in the world. If you did, you would side with us, but you heel to Everard like the mutts you are. Not a royal one among you."

I barked a harsh laugh.

"Walden, I've no love for you or yours. I'd kill Usorin, given the opportunity. The man is a monster."

I dodged another series of blows from the machine. It strained against the bench in an attempt to reach me. A loud crack gave an instant's notice before the bench tore loose from the floor, crashing on its side. One of the metal legs skittered past me as I ran. Reaching down, I snatched the metal up and turned on the mechanical giant.

The blade came down at me from overhead and to the right. I swung the steel hard, aiming for the weakest point of the armament: the weld. A resounding clang announced the hit as the saw sputtered and the housing cracked. The force of the blow sent me sliding down the aisle on my back between benches. The steel leg protruded from the wrist assembly and banged against the automaton's metal body as it tried to rid itself of the extra weight.

"If you truly hate Usorin, you would join our cause, not destroy technology to maintain their power. We are the liberators."

Walden sounded like a traveling preacher telling listeners to follow him to heaven. More likely than not, he'd steal their money and run off with their wives.

Images of Ruari and the others flashed through my head. What would happen to them with people like Ovro in charge? I pushed the thoughts from my head, focusing on my mission.

"So you and your friends can take over?" I laughed. "Nothing changes except a lot of innocent people die while you overthrow Everard and take power."

With a loud crash, the leg fell loose from the machine's

wrist. The saw blade started again. Of all the bad luck, it must have shorted the circuit, not cut it. I fired a bolt of lightning at the wrist, hoping to fry the wiring, but the shot went wide, glancing harmlessly off the machine's forearm.

"You are a peasant and know nothing of the halls of power. We would represent the people with honor and fairness," Walden said from the darkened end of the workshop.

I rolled behind another bench, keeping out of reach of the automaton.

"Honor and fairness like your brother Stirling shooting Kyla in the back after their duel ended? He tried to kill me, but failed. I witnessed him burn to death while Usorin watched."

Walden stepped into the light. His face was red, and veins stood out on his forehead.

"You will not speak my brother's name. He died a hero to his cause."

He needed to be closer in order for me to get a good shot. I scoffed.

"Hero? He shot Kyla in the back after she dropped her shields, then killed a bunch of guards, all because she refused to marry him. The Watch put him down like a rabid dog."

That did it.

Walden advanced, arm out, ready to strike. I snapped off a set of darts that struck him in the leg, just above the left knee. He screamed in pain. I didn't have time to gloat as the automaton's cleaver arm slammed into my metal one, throwing me over a bench and into a wall. Breath returned to me as I slid down to the floor. My head spun a bit, but other than a huge rent in my arm directly through the alarium tubes, nothing was broken. I triggered the lightning and nothing happened, as I expected.

The automaton turned the corner and headed in my direction. The cleaver had snapped off at the wrist from the force of hitting my metal arm. I wobbled to my feet and ran toward the forge. Walden had retreated again, screaming threats in a far less controlled voice than before. A series of fireballs arched in my direction but were so poorly thrown that they didn't even come close. They did, however, show me a beautiful sight—a three-pound forging hammer.

Snatching up the hammer, I readied myself to take on the automaton. I'd had enough of magi politics and Watch missions. All I wanted was to go back to creating new devices in the shop. I needed to destroy the spinning saw if I was going to take the thing down. The machine had the blade up and ready to attack as we came together in combat. I swung the hammer at the descending blade and missed. My new arm moved faster than my natural one and the blade caught my wrist, tearing into the metal, showering sparks in great fountains above us. The hammer fell to the floor as the metal hand separated from my wrist.

I retreated backward as the blade hit the stone floor. Pointing my left arm, I unloaded all the burning darts into the automaton's head. It staggered backward as they struck, but it quickly righted itself. The blade came up for another round. I was out of ammo, missing a hand, and rapidly losing my strength. This wasn't the best day of my life.

"Down," I heard as the entry door slammed open. I dove to the floor, moving behind an anvil for protection. A dull thump of a gunshot sounded in the distance as a projectile streaked across the workshop. The resulting explosion tore the machine apart into so many bits of scrap metal. Walden screamed again before thinking better of it and running.

Roland had arrived, and I'd be answering for this mess before long.

9

"Don't just stand there!" Roland yelled as I stood up from the wreckage. "Ovro has to be silenced."

When I didn't move, he said, "You swore an oath to protect Astaria. You've a job to do, so get doing it."

I swallowed down the anger and fear, knowing Roland was right. I'd promised to protect the people of Astaria and Ovro was a threat. Walden had gone through the forge. I ran, gaining speed, driven by Roland's betrayal of my trust. I'd spent the last year with Roland and he causally threatened to kill me?

Both my weapons were broken. I'd have to find something to use against him. I followed the blood spots left by Walden's leg and discovered a secret door that led outside. I really didn't want to kill him in public, even in the middle of the night. He couldn't be moving fast on a torn-up leg, so I ghosted from building to building in pursuit.

I ducked into an alley as I heard two male voices, slurred with drink, singing off-key as they stumbled past. I slid out behind them, increasing my speed. From the maps I'd seen,

Walden was headed toward the Ovro mansion, and I'd never get him if he reached it.

The thought of killing in cold blood made me queasy. Walden attacked me because I'd been sent to destroy the automaton. If Walden hadn't been waiting for me, I'd have blown the building and headed back to the workshop to create new devices and gear. Damn Walden straight to hell for messing this up.

I reached the corner of the town center and stopped. Walden lay on the cobblestones, grasping his leg. The damage the darts did was far more than I'd expected. I advanced on the downed man, unsure what to do.

He looked up, resigned fury etched across his face.

"Just like a commoner. You could do me the mercy of an easy death but no, you make me run across town like some mongrel escaping the hunt."

I moved closer to him, unsure how to end this man. I'd never killed anyone before. I'd assumed anyone I had to kill would be like Roland had done with Stirling. I'd regained my arm and had a new life, and now the bill had come due. Ruari always said nothing came for free, especially for people like us, while the magi could do as they pleased with little consequence. Well, today I was Walden's payback.

Three muffled explosions sounded behind me. Roland must have blown the workshop and the automaton to scraps, which meant I needed to finish this fast.

Walden sighed.

"If you're thinking I'll fight back, you are sadly mistaken. You'll have to kill me in cold blood, just like your kind did Stirling. You call us the monsters, yet you kill at the behest of the Arch Magus's slightest whim."

"I'm not a killer."

Well, at least I wasn't *yet*. I stared at the broken magus and all I saw was a high-falutin' man, not some oppressor.

Walden sneered. "It certainly looks that way from here. Just fry me and be done with it, or help me and I'll make it so you can take your place in the new order once Everard is overthrown."

Hope sprang to life in his eyes as I stood still. Either side offered the same thing—death and power at the expense of everyone else. Supporting Walden wouldn't make the commoners' lives better. It wouldn't give parents more food for their kids, or make it safer to be around the magi.

I shook my head slowly. Having taken on the mantle of the Watch, I didn't have to like it, but I had to finish it. I stepped over to Walden.

"I'm sorry," I said, watching his face crumble.

"You can shove your—"

I slammed my broken arm down into his exposed throat. The jagged edged tore through the flesh like a saw. Blood spattered me as I struck again and again until he was dead. I stood, retrieved the Watch coin from my pocket, and left it on the corpse.

Roland stood behind me as I turned. A smug look of satisfaction crossed his face.

"It'll get easier from here out, lad. The first time is always the worst."

It wouldn't. My metal arm cost far more than I ever thought it would. The blood would wash away, but I doubted the feeling ever would. Maybe if I threw myself into my work, I'd forget for a while. I followed as Roland made his way back to the safe house.

Hovel was the word I'd use for it. After climbing a set of rickety stairs that groaned under our weight, Roland forced the door open. Thankfully, the interior was far cleaner than the rest of the building. I unlatched my arm, which still trailed bits of Walden's flesh, and dropped it to the floor. I'd have to build a new one to replace it. Grabbing a pitcher of water, I set to cleaning the blood off my face and body, which was far harder to do with only one hand, but I made do. After I changed out of my filthy clothes, I returned to my plain, but serviceable, outfit.

I found Roland removing the alarium cores from the broken arm and storing them in small vials that he carried in a leather satchel.

"Can't have these just lyin' around. Some fool will kill themselves, touch what they shouldn't." He looked up at me, one bushy white eyebrow arched. "So how do you think it went?"

I grunted as I dropped into a chair near the fireplace. The night had been a mess. I'd been forced to kill a man who was no more my enemy than Roland—who'd threatened to kill me.

"Bit of a disaster from where I sit, lad." He removed another piece of alarium from the chamber and repeated the process. I still wore the gauntlet that fired the burning darts, unable to remove it without assistance. "Why didn't you just throw the bombs and run?"

"If Walden hadn't been there, I would have, but I didn't know if he could disarm them. Would have looked bad to hand over three sets of explosives to a man bent on killing Everard."

"True," he said after a moment. "I hadn't thought of that. I guess we should have loaded you up with shields, but they are awkward and heavy to wear on stealth missions."

"Walden said they are grouping to overthrow the Arch Magus."

Roland snickered.

"They are always plotting to overthrow him. Fact of the matter is that Everard is one of the few true wizards left in the realm. These jumped-up dandies don't have the fortitude to become real wizards, so they settle for our bits and baubles. Much easier."

"But together they could overthrow him easily. What is one man against a hundred?"

Roland finished removing the alarium from my old arm, which he sat on the floor.

"Lad, when I was young and first taken into Everard's service, the seafaring Norns landed on the beaches of Perlugia. Lord Magus Jul held the city for three days. The raiders were all but set to breach the walls and plunder the keep when Everard appeared. The Arch Magus has real magic, not the gizmos we give the magi. He stood atop the walls and used his magic. The earth itself was torn asunder and swallowed half their army. Waves tore ships apart like they were made of twigs. Men burst into flames as they ran from battle. That is why they will never move against Everard."

I sat in stunned silence. I'd thought I understood the situation, but I didn't, not by a long shot. How could anyone counter such power with alarium-fueled devices? No wonder the Watch fell in line with Everard.

"I see you understand why we do what we do. If a group rises up against the Arch Magus, it will be wholesale slaughter, and we can't allow that. We protect the people from Everard; not him from them."

He leaned back in his chair and watched as I came to grips with that.

"What about Usorin?"

His eyes narrowed as he answered.

"What about him?"

"Is he a wizard? Can he be killed?"

Roland sternly repeated, "Usorin is off-limits, even to us. Understand?"

"Understood."

Just because I agreed now, didn't mean that I always would.

One day I'd get even with Usorin.

10

Two weeks passed as I rebuilt my fighting arm. Given the damage it had taken, I needed to rethink the structure. After a few failed attempts, I moved the internal alarium reservoir to the forearm and built in the ability to throw flame or shoot lightning. In the left-hand gauntlet, I changed out the darts to contain a knockout powder that could incapacitate bystanders without harming them. I wanted to avoid killing innocents.

Jabber brought me meals and reminded me to sleep occasionally. The automaton butler was a reassuring presence amongst the troubles of everything else. I thought about Ruari and the boys back at the smithy. I wondered if Ruari's wife sent down breakfast for Alarik now that I was gone. My heart ached with loneliness as I worked away at Treetop.

The last piece I worked on was the shield pack. The generator weighed about six pounds and ran from my shoulders to my lower back. It was designed so the appearance would be minimal when worn under a robe. The Watch was touchy about looking like hunchbacks in public. Given time,

I might be able to make changes, but it would do for now. I wired in the switch to the left gauntlet for activation.

My next mission came a few days later. Roland and I packed up the gear and rode to the port city of Cheim. In the long past, Cheim had been the major city in Terralon, but centuries of Norn raiding parties had convinced the ruling class to move inland. Cheim had fallen to the wolves, leaving only a husk behind. The wharves and dockside were a mixture of dilapidated stone buildings and thrown-together wooden shacks built from the scraps of raiders' ships. Its keep still stood guard at the bay's entry, cannons pointed outward to discourage invaders. The raids were smaller now and less frequent, but the citizens lived with the specter of past atrocities.

As we crested the last hill into Cheim, Roland pointed out our destination. The merchants' guild had constructed a fortified ring just off the docks which they used as a clearing house for the goods that flowed in and out of port. The wall stood fifteen feet high with higher platforms for Usorin's magi to defend from if needed. Four large warehouses, boarding houses, brothels, and trading venues were arranged in a neat and orderly fashion inside the compound. The cobblestoned streets were wide enough for teams of horses to travel two abreast.

The guard on watch reviewed the paperwork Roland provided, which claimed we were there to pick up spices for one of the Bradenbridge merchants.

We rolled through the gate and into the relative safety of the merchants' retreat.

"Interesting set-up," I observed, pushing my hat back as we rolled through the nearly empty streets. "Hard to believe illegal tech is coming through here."

Roland chuckled. "Illegal *everything* comes through here,

lad. Where there's gold to be made, there will always be men willing to risk the pirates and bandits for the reward."

I nodded, keeping my eyes moving, watching for trouble. In broad daylight, I doubted people saw us as more than what they wanted to believe we were; master transporter and his apprentice. After dark, we wouldn't be seen at all—if we were lucky.

We stabled behind the boarding house. I toted the trunk with our mission gear inside. The entry was decorated with a wreath of flowers that smelled of lavender. A kindly, older woman, her gray hair pulled into a bun, met us at the door.

"Welcome to the Port's Side, Master Rathion."

Her eyes wandered over me a bit more than I'd have liked. Rawhide gloves covered the metal hand of my fighting arm under my thick, linen shirt.

"And this be?"

"Madam Esbeth, this be my man, Qix. He's me new apprentice," Roland said; his voice held a thick, nautical accent. "I'm teachin' him the ropes."

Her eyes went between us appraisingly.

"Will he be needin' his own room?"

"Nah, hardy boy like this'll be sleepin' on the floor. He doubles as my bodyguard."

She frowned slightly at that. "Big lad like that should have his own room. I'd charge ya half a coin for a small room under the rafters."

"Much obliged, but I like him near."

Roland pulled a gold coin from his pouch. He took Esbeth's hand, placed the coin in it, curled her fingers around it and then kissed them. "That should cover all our expenses for the next two days."

Her smile returned like the sun from behind fleeing clouds.

"Indeed, it shall. I had your normal room made up for ya.

I'll have Gerome take a straw pallet up for the boy. No extra charge."

"That'd be mighty nice of ya."

Roland followed the woman into the house and up the stairs to the second floor. She unlocked the door and handed him the key.

"Supper be ready in about an hour. Fish stew and fresh rolls tonight."

"We'll be down," Roland said, bowing to the landlady as she retreated down the stairs. I set the trunk at the foot of the bed before stretching my back out. The room held a large bed, a wash basin with a towel and washcloth set next to it, and a mirror hanging over it. A small chest of drawers and a writing desk finished off the room. There were no windows, so the light came from a mudstone lamp that hung next to the bed.

"Let's stretch our legs and see what's about," Roland said. He straightened his coat, covering the knife and pistol he concealed. "Something is bothering me about this place, so keep your eyes open.

"It could be the fish stew." I raised my hands in surrender as his glare fixed on me.

"Not funny, but we'll eat somewhere else, just the same."

We left the Port's Side and ventured down the lane toward the gambling houses and brothels. The whole enclave was set up to pick as much gold out of the merchants' pockets as fast as they'd made it. The clouds that scudded in were pregnant with rain—a bad sign for my mission tonight. I pulled the rim of my hat lower to shield my eyes as we passed through the gambling district. There were a few groups of men about, sticking close together, speaking in low, hushed tones. The air filled with a tension I couldn't put my finger on.

"Is it always like this?"

Roland barley shook his head.

"No, it's usually full of people, gold flowing and the streets full of noise. Something is very wrong."

We continued to walk in silence, leaving the gambling behind. The merchant houses were on the far side of the warehouses, insulating the wealthy from the common ruffians. Roland directed us to a small door in the third warehouse. He pounded on the door with the side of his hand. A moment later a large, burly man with a long, brown beard and not many teeth emerged.

"What do you want?" he snarled at Roland.

"I'm here to pick up a package from Julaan. He's expecting me."

Roland's demeanor looked relaxed, but I could see the tension in his shoulders as he prepared to fight if needed.

"Gone," the other said lazily. "Two days ago, he no show for work. Not seen him since."

Roland retrieved a piece of paper from his pocket.

"Can you get this package for me?"

"Ya." He looked us up and down. "Might take a while."

Roland spun a silver coin on the back of his knuckles, catching the man's attention. He flipped it into the air. The big man swiped at it but missed as it disappeared into Roland's palm.

"Gotta be quick to catch the coin."

The man grunted but left in a hurry. We stood there for a while before the door reopened. He thrust the paper at Roland.

"Nuthin' there."

Roland scowled, but spun the coin into plain view and handed it to the man.

"Thank you for checking, my good man."

He pivoted on his heel and walked back the way we came. I followed behind, unsure of what had just happened. As I opened my mouth to ask, Roland held up his hand. "I'll explain when we can talk freely."

I didn't ask, just followed as we walked around the rest of the enclave. Up ahead I saw something that stopped my heart cold. I grabbed Roland and pulled him back as Walden Ovro crossed the street in front of us.

In the name of all that was holy, how had he returned from the dead?

11

R oland spun, pulling me along with him as we increased the distance between us and the man I had killed.

"He was dead, I swear," I whispered to Roland.

"I know, lad; I saw your handiwork. Something is seriously amiss around here."

He led us the long way back to the Port's Side and up into our room. The pallet had been delivered and set off to the side by the desk. I checked the lock on the trunk, but it hadn't been touched as far as I could tell.

"I tore his head almost completely from his shoulders. He shouldn't be walking around by the light of day. So how does a man I killed come back to life?" I asked, trying to keep the panic out of my voice.

Roland dropped hard on the bed. "I saw his body. He was dead." He rubbed his face, looking more like an old man than I'd ever seen before.

"I've got no answers for ya, lad. I wish I did. If the Ovro have struck a deal with the devil himself, I have no idea how to stop it."

I sat on the edge of the truck.

"What do we do now? Can we call in others to help, or Everard himself?"

The idea of the Arch Magus unleashing his power against his own people frightened me, but not nearly as much as the dead coming back to life.

"If Walden is here, then he's expecting me."

Roland nodded slowly. "He's expecting you, but he's not expecting *us*. You follow the mission as laid out tonight. I'll go ahead and set up near the target. You come in the front door and I'll kick in the back. He'll never know what hit him."

We spent the next hour getting Roland equipped with one of the new alarium bombs we'd developed. It looked more like an empty scabbard then a bomb. We'd changed the triggering mechanism so it could be set and dropped to cover our tracks. The rest of his kit was different from mine, so I wasn't sure what he could do in addition to throwing fire. He pulled a too large, brown, homespun cloak on over his gear and left.

Over the next six hours I disassembled, cleaned, and reassembled the gear I brought, my hands going through the routine I'd honed over the past year. I'd tested the gear in my right arm enough to make sure it worked, but I wanted to eliminate any possible problems in the rest before I faced Walden Ovro again. I watched the clock that I'd set up next to the bed: three hours until I needed to head out. Overhead, I heard the peal of thunder. The mission would be tough enough without rain, but as they said, man plans and God laughs.

I laid out my gear, then laid back on the bed. Eyes closed, I rehearsed each part of the plan: climbing over the wall, the path to the abandoned factory, and the assent into where my target was. The Arch Magus's people had heard rumors of

Norn's bringing in illegal tech through the port. My job was to kill anyone there and retrieve or destroy anything I found. Straight-forward enough, unless there were thirty armed Norns or one undead Walden Ovro waiting for me.

When the time came, I readied myself quickly, moving with a practiced efficiency that the long months of training had drilled into me. I might not be a natural killer like Roland, but I had the gear down. The last piece to go on was the Watch mask.

I slid from our room and opened the door across from us. Roland had ensured the room was empty so we could leave via the window. I pushed the shutters open and lowered myself to the ledge that ringed the first floor. From there, it was a short jump down to the cobblestones. The shock from landing was more painful than expected but didn't slow me down as I moved into the night.

The gusting winds picked at the cloak I wore, but thankfully the ankle straps held the corners and middle so it didn't billow out behind me. Following the directions I'd memorized, I came to the apothecary shop that sat next to the enclave wall. Roland had chosen this spot as it prevented anyone seeing me go over.

The rain started as I pulled on the spiked glove I needed for the climb. I'd affixed toe-grips to my boots earlier to help me over the rough-slab stone wall. The winds howled as I set my grips and climbed. Lightning flashed overhead, and the long, low boom of thunder answered his sister's call. The water sluiced down the wall, weakening my grip as the packing between the stones loosened, but I made it to the top, looking more like a drowned rat than a man. Going down proved easier as the wall shielded me from the worst of the storm.

I made my way along the base of the wall until I spotted the dirt track that led down into the old port section of

Cheim. Most of the buildings stood empty except for beggars and others down on their luck. I edged around an animal pen and crouched to examine the target. The stone building stood solid amidst the other decay. With the lightning flashing around the sky I could make out details of the upper floors. The windows had been boarded over, but cracks of light stood out in the darkness between lightning strikes.

The rain made me slower than normal, but it saved my life. I stopped short of the entry to wait out the next lightning flashes when I spotted a large man in the alcove beside the door. The rain had drawn his beard out like a hammered out billet. At just over seven feet, he was as imposing a figure as I'd ever seen. The intel was correct—Norns were in Cheim.

I stayed out of sight, eyes closed until the next flash passed, not trusting the mask's goggles to compensate for the changes in brightness. I wondered if Ruari would be proud of the man I'd become thought I somehow doubted it. I pushed the thoughts away and focused. Ducking low, I charged the guard who couldn't see me due to the aftereffects of blinding light.

It almost worked.

I punched low, aiming for the man's family jewels, when he reacted. My fist glanced off the flat of the axe head he'd held in front of him. A dull clang was the only effect of my strike.

Faster than I'd believed possible, he flipped the axe head up, catching me in the gut with the top of the weapon. The air whooshed from my lungs. His huge boot followed, slamming into my chest and throwing me backwards into the mud.

Some assassin I was. I'd failed to take out an un-expecting man.

He raised the war axe over his head with a shout, ready to

cleave through me. The weapon descended, only to be stopped as my shield sprang up between us. He pulled back for another chop with a startled grunt, but I threw a ball of fire into his face. With all that hair, he'd have been a torch on a dry day, but as wet hair covered most of his face, it only left him a bit singed.

I rolled out of the way of the second strike, hearing the axe head squelch in the mud as it struck. It took him a moment to pull the head free, and I took that opportunity to lash out with a kick to his arm as he pulled back. Blood showered down from where the teeth of my boot grips bit into his flesh. He bellowed in rage, one-handedly whipping the freed axe at my head.

Instead of retreating, I dodged the swing and grabbed him. I felt the spikes of my climbing gloves bite into his arm just as I fired a burst of lightning. Wet skin and metal barbs made for an excellent conductor, and the energy crackled through the contacts into him. A moment later, he dropped over dead, taking me with him.

It took a bit to peel my metal hand out of the glove that had melted into the Norn's skin. Once free, I dragged him through the driving rain, leaving him out of sight. The mission had just started, and I'd already killed a man. My stomach sank at the thought of more killing as the prospects of this being an easy mission faded.

I forced myself to continue through my dread. I felt no love toward our ancestral enemies, but this had become about protecting the people of Astaria. If the Norn helped overthrow Everard, it would open the way to war, a war I wasn't sure we could win with Walden Ovro leading us.

A steel-banded oak door stood before me. I could still run. Roland could probably handle this without me; instead, I hardened my nerves. I'd taken on the mantle of the Watch and I intended to see it through, if only to protect the people of Bradenbridge.

I opened the door to disaster.

W alden Ovro stood in the center of the room with three others. Two were Norn men, huge behemoths like the one I'd just killed. The third was Roland. He hung limply between the massive Norns, blood dripping from his face. I could see the Watch mask laying at his feet. He looked up at me, his eyes unfocused, but he was awake. His head dropped back as he feigned uncon- sciousness. If I did nothing else, I'd save Roland, I promised myself.

The large room held three long tables, each laid out with workshop tools. Candles and shuttered lamps were placed around the room to provide enough light to see by but not to escape the boarded-up windows and invite inspection. Three people sat huddled at the far table working frantically as they cast worried glances at the Norns. A staircase ran up to the second floor where the devices were stored. Once again, Walden had laid the trap for me to walk into.

"So good of you to join us, Watcher Quinn," Walden purred as I stepped out of the rain. His voice had a raspy quality it hadn't before. A small price to pay after having your throat ripped out. "Your associate was not so forth-coming with information, but we persuaded him."

"How are you still alive?" I asked before I could stop myself. In stressful situations, my mouth went to places that my brain knew better not to.

"Ah, the wonders of Norn shaman magic." Ovro pulled down the high collar on the blue coat he wore. There, in the guttering candlelight, I saw livid, red stitching. "You did a fine job of slashing my throat, but you didn't sever my spine, so they were able to put me back together. It was exquisitely painful, but I am alive."

"I should have done a better job," I mumbled, but he either didn't hear me or ignored it altogether. The Norns glowered at me and I wondered if they knew I'd killed their mate.

"It is so nice that when I whistle you come running like a puppy," Ovro said to me as he approached. I tensed, ready to strike as he closed the distance. "You so much as flinch and they'll tear his arms out before you get a shot off, boy."

I relaxed my arm, gaining a smile from Walden as he studied me. Should I risk it and try to free Roland, I wondered, or wait and see what happens? Once they removed my arm, I'd be severely hindered but, more impor-tantly, I'd be handing over all our new devices. Roland had been ready to kill me if I hadn't tried to kill Ovro. Should I act differently?

"Excellent. It is good to deal with a rational man for a change." Walden stepped closer, locking eyes with me. "I offered you a place with us before, and you were very rude in your response, but I am prepared to forgive and forget. We need an experienced artificer to help us overthrow Everard. Usorin will be the new Arch Magus and lead Astaria to its proper place in the world."

"And where would that be?" a snarly voice asked from the

top of the stairs. The largest man I'd ever seen stomped down the stairs, eliciting squawks of fear from the three at the table. His massive shoulders held a bearskin cloak that must have weighed as much as me. A huge axe hung from his belt, along with a wicked, curved dagger. His beard came to the middle of his chest. The most frightening part of him, though, were his glacial blue eyes that pierced through me as he took me in.

Walden wiped the shocked expression off his face before turning toward the hulking Norn.

"Throndor, just trying to entice the young Quinn to join us in ridding the world of Everard once and for all."

Throndor pushed past Walden, causing the smaller man to stumble before righting himself.

"Boy, did you kill my man outside?"

I stopped myself from stepping backwards. The Norn reeked of sweat, beer, and fish, causing my stomach to roil.

"Yes."

He leaned in close enough that I could see the veins in his eyes and missed the earlier stench quite a bit. Spittle flickered across my face as he spoke.

"What's to stop me from killing you, then?"

Walden stepped between us, pushing me back.

"Throndor, we discussed that having a member of the Watch join our ranks would ease the task of ridding ourselves of Everard. The members are the only ones allowed to see him anymore, since his paranoia has grown to such levels."

"He's not paranoid," I said softly. "The Arch Magus knows there is a plot in play to remove him."

Walden gestured in my general direction.

"The boy speaks with the wisdom of youth. If we try to attack his keep, he'll have time to unleash his magic against us. A single Watch guard could enter and assassinate him. He'd never see it coming."

My brain kicked into action, putting the pieces together, building a new design from the parts at hand. "You'd need Roland for that as well."

"What?" Throndor asked, his deep voice reverberating around the room. "I'm not stupid enough to leave two of you alive. If we only need that one," he jerked his thumb back at Roland who played the unconscious man, "then I can kill you for the death of Gorestun."

"He won't murder the Arch Magus," I said, staring at the larger man. "But I might. I can't do it dead."

Walden's eyes narrowed.

"Why the sudden change of heart? You refused last time and slayed me."

"Last time, Roland threatened to kill me if I didn't finish you," I said as calmly as I could. I'd never been much of a liar, but I thought of Tur and hoped his example would be enough. There had to be a way out of this mess that didn't get one of us killed. Ruari always told me to bide my time and keep my eyes open, and I'd see the right path when it came. I had my eyes wide open. "I didn't want to die then, and I don't want to die now."

Throndor looked disgusted.

"Have you no honor or loyalty to your brothers? What kind of man would trade his own just to save his own skin? Kill him and be done with this."

Walden held up his hands. "A useful man is what we have here. How many Norns did Everard destroy on the beaches during the red tide?"

"He destroyed over forty clans of fighters. The wails of their women can still be heard in the caverns of loss," Throndor said, his face pale as his eyes lost their focus. "My father and brothers died that day. I swore a vengeance pact to make him pay."

"Exactly," Walden said, his voice brimming with confidence. He turned back to me. "Why do you need Roland?"

A reason. I needed a reason for needing Roland. Walden's eyes took on a calculating expression as I thought.

"Well?"

"I haven't been presented as an official member of the Watch, as killing you was my initiation. Next week, I am to be brought before the Arch Magus to be sworn in." Tur would be proud of that whale of a story. It may have sounded a bit rushed; I fought the urge to blurt it out.

Ovro smiled. "And there, my friend Throndor, is the opening we need. Young Quinn goes in with Roland, kills Everard and Usorin takes over. Norn and Astaria become allies and conquer the rest of the world."

"This smells like the bilge of a scow. Once he goes in, he could warn Everard." Throndor shook his head ponderously. "No, we need another way."

"I haven't mentioned my payment for killing the Arch Magus." I crossed my arms and waited as the two exchanged glances. This had caught them off-guard, and the path became clear to me.

"What is your price, boy?" Throndor asked impatiently. His hand strayed to the head of his axe. The two Norns holding Roland moved to pull their weapons.

I prepared to act if this went bad, though I doubted I could beat Throndor on my best fighting day, ever.

"I want to kill Usorin."

The room went dead silent.

13

Throndor broke the silence with a mighty laugh that bounced around the room. His men echoed the laughter as he continued, though I doubt they knew why they were laughing.

"This boy should have been a Norn. He's got brass nuggets in his pants. Kill Usorin." His laughter redoubled at the thought.

Walden didn't laugh; instead, he eyed me with stern dissatisfaction.

"Enough. Usorin is our leader, he isn't payment for killing Everard."

Throndor got himself under control and his men followed his lead. "Tell me why you would kill Usorin."

I didn't have to fake emotion this time or even think about what to say. It shocked me to realize how much anger I'd buried as I worked with Roland. I held out my right arm and pulled up the sleeve to expose the metal. "He cut off my arm and I'll have his head in payment for it. I was a blacksmith, and he ruined my life."

That stopped them cold. I could feel the rage flowing

through me as I spoke, knew that it seeped out of every pore of my skin like heat from a forge. I wanted the bastard dead, but stopping Ovro and the Norns was much more important. I silently hoped they bought it.

"You can't kill Usorin. Who would we prop up on the throne?" Walden whined, as his hand rubbed absently at his neck where I'd nearly decapitated him. "He is the only one powerful enough to hold off the others while we consolidate power."

"So Usorin isn't part of this?" I asked confusedly. The way Walden spoke, I'd thought he was an active participant in the plot against Everard.

"Usorin? Please." Walden sniffed indignantly. "The man's sack is as is empty as the meanest peasant's purse. Everard lets him do anything as long as the alarium flows."

Throndor nodded. "We must hold the mines at all cost." He turned to me. "You may ask another boon, but Usorin will not be part of the bargain."

The path opened before me as clear as day.

"I want to see Roland, make sure you haven't injured him badly enough to stop my presentation."

"What price will you ask?" Throndor's massive hand stopped me from reaching Roland. "I'd know if we have a pact before you see your master."

"Oh, let him look at the old man, Throndor," Ovro said with a huff. "All this gets tiresome. Quinn will be rewarded for his betrayal and we will complete our plans together."

The hand moved off my shoulder. I glanced at the giant, who studied me carefully. The Norns looked stupid, but Throndor obviously wasn't. I reached Roland and pushed his chin up. One eye had swollen, but didn't appear too bad. "Can you stand on your own?"

"I can."

I looked over my shoulder. "Throndor, tell your men to let him go."

A darkness covered the giant's face, but he motioned his men away. They glared at me as they dropped Roland's arms. They took a couple of steps back, but their hands never left their weapons. I made a show of checking Roland over. They'd stripped him of all his gear, but I hoped they'd overlooked one piece. I probed his stomach, which caused him to wince in pain, but my left hand found the alarium detonator.

"Enough," Throndor bellowed. "You've checked your man and he'll live. Now answer my question. What will it take for you to kill Everard?"

I pulled the bomb free of Roland's belt and depressed the trigger.

"It will be a cold day in hell before I'll kill Everard for you."

I tossed the bomb to the floor at Throndor's feet. I lurched up and forward, grabbing Roland as I triggered the full shield.

Walden screamed.

"Bomb!"

He turned and ran from the room. Throndor kicked the bomb at me but it ricocheted off the shield. A moment later it detonated. The room flared with light as the bomb exploded. Both Norn guards vanished as the light hit them.

The goggles protected my eyes from the flash. My shield strained to absorb the impact of the blast, but it was strong enough to knock us from our feet. The shield cut out as we landed.

"That was your plan?" Roland shouted over the fire and creaking timbers. "Remind me to let them kill me next time."

The room was completely engulfed in flames; the beams above us had cracked as the weight from above strained the damaged wood. A loud crack warned us we didn't have a lot of time, or options. I pushed Roland toward the staircase that hadn't collapsed yet. I'd seen windows up there earlier. We could force our way out.

"Go, we can get out from up there."

"Are you crazy, lad? The floor's about to go!" he shouted as I pushed him.

"Better to be over it than under it."

Roland stumbled as the building lurched. I grabbed the smaller man and threw him over my shoulder. The flames on the stairs licked at my boots as I jumped awkwardly over the lower steps. I pulled myself upright and took the rest two at a time. Part of the floor gave way, smashing the stairs as we reached the landing.

Smoke flowed upwards, the stairs acting like a chimney. Reaching the second floor provided some relief from the fire. I saw the boarded-up window and moved toward it. More of the floor gave way behind us as the fire raged out of control. I kicked out a couple of boards, glad to see them tumble away into the darkness. I shouldered a few more boards out until there was enough room for us to climb through.

Another explosion rocked the building as the fire claimed the old structure. In the distance, I thought I could make out people running toward the inferno, but I couldn't concentrate on anything but getting away from there. It was a fifteen-foot drop to the old road below. Alone, I might have managed it, but not with Roland. I cursed the loss of my climbing glove, but would have to chance the rain-slick stones as it continued to pour.

I set Roland on his feet.

"Can you hang onto my back?" I asked, and got a shallow nod in return. The older man wrapped his arms around my neck. I could feel the heat flare as the fire consumed the far side of the floor as it crashed down. I idly wondered if the people at the tables downstairs had made it out.

The first step was almost my last as the stone crumbled underfoot as I put our combined weight on the sill. My left climbing glove bit into the wet rock and held, allowing me to steady myself. With an outward swing, I got my right foot onto a piece of the ledge that looked more solid. It held as I let go of the breath I'd been holding. Water sluiced down my face as I edged to the rear corner of the building. Voices rose up from below as someone spotted us.

A dozen steps later, I hung from the crenelated columns that decorated the old building. I started down, feet occasionally slipping on the wet stone or when Roland shifted. I knew his strength was limited and worked fast. We reached the bottom, and I put my arm under Roland and moved us away from the building just as the roof collapsed above us. A shower of bright embers lived and died, quickly extinguished in the driving rain.

We'd walked into another trap and somehow survived it. I doubted they'd give me a third chance to kill Everard—not that I wanted to. The Norns' involvement puzzled me. Why prop up a false leader instead of just conquering what they wanted? The warriors of Norn were renowned for their swift strikes, pillaging, and raiding along the coasts. Why wouldn't they want to rule Astaria?

I kept us moving into the wet night, keeping away from witnesses to the disaster. I needed to get Roland as far from Cheim as possible while he was injured. When we reached the stable behind the Port's Side, I helped him into the wagon. A quick trip to retrieve our gear and provisions for the road went unnoticed.

I returned to the stable to see Roland had the wagon ready to go. He caught my eye as I came in.

"You did good, lad. Thought we were dead men there for a bit."

I stored the gear in the back of the wagon before Roland

eased himself onto the spring seat. He released the lever as I climbed on and we rolled out into the storm.

I stared off into the distance as he drove us to the enclave's gate. A flash of lightning showed me a tall man staring from an alley. By the second flash of lightning, he was gone.

Throndor had survived the explosion.

14

We arrived back at Treetop in the middle of our second day out of Cheim. I'd backtracked to ensure that we hadn't been followed, though the odds were unlikely. I couldn't decide if I'd actually seen Throndor standing in the rain or if I'd imagined it. In the light of day, it made no sense that he would let us go.

I brought the trunk up on the lift and stored it in the workshop. Most of Roland's gear was gone, most likely melted down in the fire. It would take weeks to rebuild what the artificer had constructed. Roland stepped into the shop.

"Lad, we need to talk."

I finished putting away the gear, carefully stowing each piece. I hadn't taken mine off since we'd left Cheim.

"Go ahead." I sat at the end of the workbench and began removing my left gauntlet. The shield had held far better than expected, which pleased me. My skills had increased at a far faster pace during my time with Roland than they ever had learning from Ruari. I still missed him and my smithy family, but I knew I could never go back without putting them in danger.

"Quinn, you did an outstanding job freeing us from Ovro and the Norns," he said as he sat across the corner from me. As I removed pieces, he took an old rag and wiped each down before setting them back in front of me. We fell into an easy rhythm of work as I dismantled the gauntlet.

"Didn't have much choice. I couldn't let them kill you. Where would I find another mentor and friend?"

I removed the housing that held the shield generator in place. Not a spot on it; the new design was solid. "How in the hell are the Norns involved in overthrowing Everard?"

Roland shook his head. "I don't understand it myself, but we've got to find and kill Ovro before it goes any further."

"So far, I haven't had much luck with killing him." I laughed. "A year ago, the only thing I ever killed was a pint of ale."

"I could use a few of those now, truth be told." Roland inspected the optic lens from the shield with a jeweler's loop before putting it down. "Not even a stress flaw in the glass. That was a handy piece of engineering."

"It held. Wasn't sure it would take a full alarium blast, but I didn't see another way out."

"You could have agreed to kill Everard," he said softly. "Quinn, I know you don't like what we do, but it is necessary."

That got my attention. I stared back at the man, wondering if he was crazy or just delusional. Maybe he'd been alone in the woods for too many years and he'd cracked.

"'Necessary' is an interesting way of describing it. Killing to maintain Everard's control over Astaria is *necessary*? If he's such a great leader, why are his subjects living in fear of the magus? Why are men like Usorin allowed to maim and walk away without consequence? Without the alarium devices we provide them with, the people could fight back and be free instead of living at the whim of crazy men."

He set down the jeweler's loop and regarded me calmly.

"Do you think corruption is the sole governance of the magi? Do you think if we elevated normal men to power, they would not take more than is theirs? In Rukland, the strongest warrior rules. Do you think they are fair to the lesser among them?" he asked.

"But a man can be beaten by strength or wit. Anyone could stand against a leader and prevail," I said, feeling the heat rise up through my face.

Roland barked a condescending laugh.

"You think they let the strong survive long enough to fight them? They take all the women and breed huge families. Boys born outside these families are killed as threats to the Rukland ways. Astaria has been at peace for years because Everard is strong enough to deter the other nations. With him gone, we would become pawns of the Norn or worse, the Candalarian Hordes. Do you think living under the Hordes' leaders would be an easy life?"

I didn't answer, having been baited into rhetorical arguments by Roland far too many times. Everything boiled down to the Astarians being unable to maintain control without the "magic" of the magus there as a shield against outside forces. I removed the outer wrist guard and cleaned the sweat and blood from the inner collar.

"You know I'm right," Roland said, a bit more smugly than usual. I wondered if being captured by the Norns and needing me to rescue him had unnerved him. From what I gathered, he'd been a lone operator for the past many years, answering only to the Arch Magus. He'd developed and built most of the devices the magi families used and passed on to keep their "magic" secret.

"No," I replied after a few moments. "We could supply an

army with the same devices and protect the country from other nations. We are technologically superior to any country, including the Norns."

He held up his hand. "You are correct, except the alarium we use is not easily obtainable, nor is it plentiful. Astaria has twelve fiefdoms, each with under ten magi and then only three or four have gear to become a magus. When one dies, the next in line learns the secret, takes up the mantle and the rule continues. No civil wars, no inheritance fights. Just the simple transfer of power."

"No, what we have is power-hungry families trampling the commoners to maintain their status. Usorin cut my arm off after *he* made a mistake."

"Boy, you need to get over that." When I began to protest, he held up a hand to stop me. "Let me speak. Usorin is a maniac and we both know it, but he is useful and controls the alarium without issue. Now, I'm not condoning what he did to you, but revenge for a missing limb does not equate to killing the man and risking a war."

"He ruined my life and probably killed many others, Roland," I shot back. "He took everything from me."

Roland looked around the room exaggeratedly. "Doesn't look ruined from where I'm sitting. In fact, you might say it's improved, given your position in the Watch and expert skills as a smith and artificer. You'd never have gotten this kind of training from Ruari."

I couldn't argue with that. I thought about living in the bunkhouse at the forge with nothing of my own. Not that I had a lot of possessions here either, but it felt like I belonged here. One day, I'd have owned Ruari's forge, though I would also have been held hostage to Usorin's whims. Would that have been a satisfactory life? The only true downside was my adopted family thought me dead and, in a way, the Quinn I'd been was truly buried.

When I didn't respond, Roland took a deep breath and released it. He left the room and returned with a bottle and two brass mugs. He unstopped the bottle, poured some amber liquid into each glass, and handed one to me. "We could both use a drink, I'm thinking."

I took the cup and swallowed the contents in one shot. The warmth of the alcohol hit my throat and spread down into my belly. The last time I'd had a drink was with Tur the night I'd tackled Stirling Ovro. That thought brought me back to what was truly important: stopping Walden Ovro and the Norns.

"How is Walden getting ahead of us?" I asked Roland as he refilled his drink. "Each time we get a mission, he's waiting there."

Roland swirled his drink as he stared into it. "As far as I can tell, he's either feeding information to the Arch Magus' people, or he's got a spy that is relating the details."

Setting the cup on the table, I returned to dismantling my gauntlet. "I feel like we are forging the wrong metals."

Roland's eyebrow quirked in surprise. "How's that, lad?"

I polished each of the pieces and laid them out before me. Apart, they were just pieces, but placed together in the proper order, the gauntlet became an asset.

"Sometimes, when you're trying to weld two metals, they just won't stick. Maybe they're dirty, maybe the metal isn't hot enough. Whatever the reason, they won't become a solid piece of metal."

"Go on," Roland said. His face had a peculiar look about it, as if he was torn between thinking I was mad or being lost by my train of thought. "I'm not sure I follow yet, but I'm curious to see where you're going."

"Not sure, myself, to be honest." I rearranged the pieces of the gauntlet, ordering them as I went.

"So, your metal won't adhere?" Roland prompted.

"When the metal won't forge, sometimes you throw it out, but often you can add flux so the weld holds, and you can craft a solid piece. What if we are missing the flux?"

"And what would we be forging?"

"A plan." I held my hands up parallel to each other. "We've got the Norns on the right and Walden Ovro on the left. No matter how much I try, I can't get a good weld between them. So, what is the flux that holds them together?"

Roland smacked the table. "Now *that's* using your brain. I hadn't looked at it like that."

I placed the guard back on my left wrist and assembled the cuff.

"They are fixated on killing Everard, but why involve us? Each time we interfere, they risk losing everything."

"Sounds like they need you. Could you be the lynch pin in their design?"

Roland poured another drink for us, but I ignored it. My hands worked to reassemble the shield device as my brain spun with the details of my meetings with Walden Ovro.

"How could they ever count on me to follow through? Everard could wipe out the Norns and the Ovros in the blink of an eye."

"You've got that right. Of course, Everard could just dispatch the Watch to do it for him."

"The Watch!" I pushed the phase regulator back into place with a sharp snap. "What is our mission?"

Both eyebrows raised at the question. "We are the artificers of the devices that protect Astaria."

I shook my head. "No, that's our mission *here*. What is the primary task of the Watch?"

"We keep order among the magi, enacting Everard's laws and punishing the transgressors," Roland said with smug satisfaction.

"But that's not how we're viewed by the magi, is it?" I felt the idea fit into place just like the outer collar of the gauntlet settling in to complete the device.

"To them, we're assassins. What does this have to do with Ovro and the Norns?"

I stood up and grabbed my mission bag. I already had my armaments, but I needed spare alarium. "That's the flux. They aren't trying to get us to do their bidding; they are trying to get us to do our job."

The trunk I'd put away earlier slid back out. I rummaged through the contents and found the spare cylinders of alarium and my toolkit. If I was right, I'd need it before all of this was done. I pushed the trunk back, threw on my robes, and headed for the lifts.

"Where do you think you're going, Quinn?"

I locked eyes with the Master Assassin.

"If I'm an assassin, then I'm going to kill."

"And just who do you do you think you'll be killing?'

"Usorin."

15

I arrived in Bradenbridge two days later under the cover of darkness. I'd had to talk fast to get Roland to stay at the workshop, but I needed him to ready his new gear more than I needed him as backup. If I was correct, my trip to Bradenbridge would confound Walden's plans and buy us time to strike.

My destination was on the far side of the arena from where Ruari's forge sat. I unsaddled the horse at the local inn and paid the groom to feed and brush him down. Afterward, I headed down the street, backtracking to make sure I hadn't been followed. I found the bakery, long since closed for the day. The root cellar door opened easily. I slid in and found the panel that opened into the hidden Watch safe house.

A small repair workbench covered one wall, the other had a small bed. I set my gear in the corner and stripped off my travel cloak. I'd need my Watch robes to pull off the plan. In order to break into Usorin's keep, I'd need to strike in the small hours of the morning when the guards would be asleep at their posts. Bradenbridge hadn't been attacked in over one hundred years, so security wasn't their highest priority.

I went through my pack, placing the alarium charges inside the wrist container I'd built into my combat arm. The next item was the baton I'd taken on my first mission; I carried it more as a talisman of good luck than for any actual need. I flipped it over in my left hand, feeling the grain of the wood, the curve of the pommel. My replacement arm functioned, but I didn't have the full range of touch that my left arm did; the fingers could sense pressure, but not fine details. I'd never be able to feel a baby's soft skin or the texture of delicate parchment ever again. I counted myself lucky to still have a useful arm, however, as being a cripple would have set me on the path of beggardom.

The workbench held a good variety of tools and I had hours to spare. I removed my combat arm and attached the utility version. It functioned, but didn't have any of the additional features. I shrugged into the harness and set to work, cleaning and calibrating my combat arm for tonight's activity. The alarium stores were full, giving me the use of fire or lightning as needed. I retrieved a pack of climbing spikes and affixed them to the fingertips. I'd find a way to retract them later, but I'd rather not have relied on gloves after what happened in Cheim. I lubricated the joints, working them back and forth to ensure a smooth range of motion. Hardened metal, like the pieces I used in the construction of the hand, could lock up if not treated properly. After all the rain and heat in Cheim, I wasn't taking any chances.

I worked without interruption, softly whistling a tune I'd heard on the night I'd met Emma. She was beyond me now, even if she'd forgiven me for tackling Ovro at the arena. My memories wandered to the forge, to Tur, Bran, and Alarik, and the days spent working together. I'd always assumed I'd become a master smith and run the forge, but a few more years with Roland and I'd be much more than a master. I'd be an artificer. The skill it took to build devices of metal and alarium far surpassed that of a normal blacksmith. Roland was right; Usorin had done me a favor, in an odd sort of way, but I'd pay him back for the inconvenience tonight.

It had taken Roland a bit to see my point, but he came around to it. Walden was being over-protective of Usorin, even at the cost of Everard's assassination and the completion of their plan. This wasn't out of loyalty; they were pushing Usorin forward as bait, knowing the only choice I'd have would be to assassinate him. I wouldn't know until I got to the keep if Walden planned to sacrifice the magus to further his plan or if I would be killed in the attempt. My guess was the latter, and that I'd be used to disband or betray the Watch.

I finished the work with hours to spare and nothing left to do. Sleep always eluded me before a mission, though I was tired. I'd eat an hour before, but for now my thoughts spun in an ever-tightening circle around what would happen in Usorin's keep. Part of me was loathe to go back to where I'd lost my arm, but at the same time it felt right to be back in Bradenbridge.

After another hour, I checked my gear for the fifth time and decided to scout the keep before the mission started. I donned the Watch mask and moved out. Any hint of what was coming could tip the scales in my favor, or at least I'd convinced myself of that.

With care, I made my way out of Bradenbridge and worked my way up the slope toward the keep. I kept low to the ground so my silhouette wouldn't give me away. After half an hour, I squatted in the tree line within sight of where Usorin had attacked me. My stomach clenched as I saw the husk of the abandoned furnace.

The scene replayed itself before my eyes. I saw Usorin pull the flame blade from the sheath and slam it down, removing my arm in a shearing slice. I imagined the arm bouncing down the hill, freed of the weight of the rest of my body. The images flashed through my head over and over as I sat with my back against a small maple tree. I saw the reddened face of the magus as he screamed over the furnace's meltdown. I'd always known Usorin to be unstable, but I hadn't realized until that day how crazy he actually was.

Finally, I pushed myself up and went to examine the furnace's remains. In the dim light, I could make out the shape I knew so well. I'd spent a month with Ruari fabricating the fire box and the boiler system for the project. Most of the box had blown apart when the alarium-fueled fire had burst through, killing Crimshaw and the rest of the magi Usorin had sent to increase the heat.

The metal had rusted in the past year of exposure, the trails standing out faintly in the twilight of my goggles. The large air ducts had been boarded up to prevent people from climbing in them. I climbed the side of the fire box and pulled the bottom board free. Whoever had secured it hadn't done a good job; the other boards were just as loose. Before me sat a tunnel that ran directly into the keep and, more importantly, Usorin's private chamber. Even if Walden and Throndor waited for me, I'd have the element of surprise on my side.

I climbed down and retreated to the tree line and watched for a bit, but no one came to investigate the increased air flow into the keep. I doubted anyone would notice the change with only one board missing and the night air lying still, but only fools took chances on faith alone.

Without needing to pass the guards stationed at the entrances to the keep, I thought about moving in sooner, but if someone discovered me and screamed, alerting the guards to my location would be just as bad as having to fight past them. Better to stick to the plan and move in the early hours.

With two hours left, I decided that I would go see the

forge one last time to say goodbye. I'd lived there most of my life and given the coming events, I wasn't sure if I'd ever get another chance.

The way down was easier, as the moon had moved behind the clouds and concealed my movements. Still, I took it slow, guarding against stray noises and other indications that I was about. The night air misted around me as I slunk down the hill, a ghost amongst the people who had once been my friends and neighbors.

I paused at the edge of Bradenbridge. What was I doing? My old life was gone, and I had nothing to gain from returning to the forge. I'd left a few small belongings from my parents in the bunk house, but I didn't know if they'd been found and thrown away. Ruari always told me that the path would become clear with thought and patience. I could see the path and knew I shouldn't take it, but I longed to see my old home, to remember what it was like to be Quinn the Blacksmith. The Watch may have saved me, but I'd lost myself in the bargain.

I steeled myself and pushed on, slowly. The last thing I needed was to be reckless and wander into the constable or a drunk who'd raise a cry in the middle of the night. I didn't need to run into Tur returning from a drunken night at the inn or a widow's house either, for that matter. Thinking of Tur's antics brought a smile to my face. He'd been like a brother to me, quick-witted and free of spirit, as my mother would have said; always a kiss for the ladies and a drink for the fellows.

The smell of horses notified me that I was close, since the farrier shop butted up to the horse stables and pens. I gave the stables a wide berth, as the young lads tended to sleep in the hay lofts. I rounded the corner and came upon the smithy. The coals were banked in the forges, dull red, waiting for air and fuel to heat the day's metal. Anvils stood just far enough away from the forge to make moving between them easy without letting the metal cool. The smell of coal greeted me like a long-lost friend. The alarium forge we used at Treetop burned hot and clean, but didn't have the smell of burning coal.

I stepped into the shop and froze. A hammer lay on the ground. I wouldn't have thought twice if this were anywhere else, but Ruari never left until everything was done up proper.

I took another step and noticed the smell of charred meat. My brain screamed at me to run, but I walked on into a scene straight out of a slaughterhouse; bodies lay on the ground around the main forge, and I grabbed the bellows' handles and pumped, igniting the coal and setting the fire to burn brighter.

The first face I saw was Alarik's. A red cloth protruded from his mouth where he'd been gagged. The boy's throat had been cut deep. Bran lay next to him, his body covered with burn marks and with a cutting tool shoved through his left eye. Tur had been gutted and left across from them. But that wasn't the worst. In the middle, chained to the anvil, was Ruari. The master smith's hands had been burned to stumps.

I wretched, glad I'd not eaten before I ventured out. This was a message for me. I'd led them to this place, and they'd killed everyone I'd ever loved. A flood of tears filled my goggles, seeping out of my mask and down my face as I stared in horror. I heard a harsh laugh behind me. I turned to face it, ready to fight.

That's when Throndor stepped out of the shadows.

16

I froze as I saw the giant. The right side of his face and shoulder bore the marks of the alarium explosion. He wore no shirt, leaving the deep pockmarks and red scars from the explosion visible in the dim light. His beard had been hacked away, leaving a jagged mess in its place. If only he'd been closer to the explosion, it would have solved that problem.

His glare pierced me as he stepped into the light of the forge.

"Why?"

I kept my eyes locked on the giant, not allowing myself to grieve for my adopted family until this was done. Throndor was a killing machine trained from birth in the hostile north, whereas I'd never been in a fight before I met Roland. How could a journeyman blacksmith and artificer hope to beat such a man?

Tur's lifeless body lay behind Throndor as he paced back and forth on the other side of the anvil. He reminded me of a cat waiting for the mouse.

"You killed my men and did this to me. I'd thought you of

all people would understand the need for revenge. All your mewling about Usorin taking your arm and you have to ask me why?"

"These people did nothing to you." I moved to keep the hulking Norn in front of me. "How did you know I'd come here?"

Throndor barked a laugh. "Walden isn't as strong as one of our women, but he is devious as a fox and mean as a ferret. He's heard of Quinn the journeyman Blacksmith. Usorin has only maimed one smith, so we knew it was you. Easy enough to hunt down your people after that."

I needed to keep him talking. I glanced around to see if Walden stood in the darkness of the smithy. "Shouldn't you be waiting for me at the keep? Isn't that where the trap is?"

Throndor pulled the heavy bladed axe from his belt. He tested the edge with his thumb, though it was for show.

"Aye, but Walden can come up with a new plan. I'm going to finish you and send you off with this paltry group. The smith was the only worthy one here." He jerked his head toward Alarik's corpse. "That one cried like a woman as I killed him. The big one fought like an old man. These lands breed pathetic sheep."

My eyes slid over the shadowed faces of my friends. They hadn't done anything wrong, yet they'd paid the price for my mistake. I'd tried to use my loss as a way to get to Walden, and he'd made me pay for my arrogance. If I got away from Throndor, I'd have to settle the score. Right then, I doubted that would ever happen. Roland would have to clean up my mess.

"Any last words before I gut you like a pig, boy?" Throndor asked as he flexed his mighty shoulders, readying to fight.

I readied the shield, knowing I'd have little room for

error. I pulled from a story I'd heard the story-teller recite in an inn.

"Can I ask a boon of you, if I fall to your blade?"

That stopped him in his tracks.

"What do you know of Norn customs to ask such a thing?"

I pushed my advantage, hoping to gain more information. "I know it is a condemned man's right to ask a favor for after he's gone. Will you honor my request?"

He eyes narrowed as he studied me. I'd obviously caught him off-guard.

"Aye, if I can. Norns do not grant foolhardy requests, and I will make your death slow and painful if you mock me."

I nodded, steadying my voice the best I could. "Will you kill Usorin for me? I want revenge for what he did."

"You would have made a fine Norn," he said slowly. "I will grant you your boon if I cross paths with Usorin after your death."

Before I could respond, Throndor leapt, bringing down the axe in a vicious, overhead arc meant to split my skull open. The shield caught the force of the blow as sparks showered from the impact. I dropped the shield and opened a spray of fire against my opponent. Throndor flinched away from the open flame, but it didn't stop him from swinging the axe at my head a second time.

The blow flew wide of me as I redirected the flames. The smell of burning hair joined the miasma of death and burnt flesh. The giant rolled on the ground as the flames fought to burn him further. Moving around the center anvil I positioned myself for another gout of flame. My arm went out to fire just as Throndor threw a handful of dirt and ash into my face.

My vision blurred as the dust covered my goggles. I could make out an indistinct shape, but couldn't see details through the dirt. My arm came up to fire another blast at the giant, but his fist slammed into the side of my head, knocking the mask from my face. I staggered from the force of the blow. Another followed, driving into my stomach and launching me into the anvil. Throndor stooped to retrieve his axe, spinning it up onto his shoulder.

"I'm going to split you right down the center like a piece of wood."

I forced air back into my lungs as I pushed off the anvil. My metal arm connected with the Norn's sternum and I heard a loud crack. Throndor backhanded me for my trouble, sending me stumbling away from him. I wobbled around to face him when Ruari saved my life. As I stepped back, my foot landed on my former master's shin and I fell backwards; Throndor spun through the air where my head had been a moment before. Even in death, Ruari still looked out for me.

I heard his laugh as Throndor stood over me.

"Not so smart now, are you?"

The Norn reared back, bringing his axe over his head. I drove my booted foot into his groin and felt the steel heads of the climbing teeth sink into flesh as it made contact. Throndor dropped the axe behind him as he clutched his ruined manhood. I turned over and climbed unsteadily to my feet.

The Norn knelt before me, gasping in pain.

"Tell me what Walden's plan is. Why does he want Usorin dead?" I asked.

Throndor didn't make a sound other than the shallow gasps of an injured man. I tapped his hands with the toe of my boot, prompting a deep groan as he bumped his injury.

"That is a painful injury. Tur over there," I pointed to where my friend lay dead on the floor. "He once fell off a wagon and hit himself right in the goods. I'm thinking at your size, it's gonna hurt a whole lot worse when I kick you a second time, though I am sorry about the spikes. Ruari always told me to never kick a man there unless I planned on killing him." I bumped his hands harder, eliciting another groan of misery. "You can tell me, or I can make you. Your choice."

He gasped again. "Usorin is a distraction from his real goal," the big man panted, as if he'd run from the keep. The already pale Norn could have been a specter with how white he was.

"What is the goal, then?" I asked, wanting to know for sure instead of being one step behind. Since this had started, Ovro had been playing a game that Roland and I weren't aware of. He had access to far more information than us and only luck and the grace of the almighty had saved us.

"I... I don't know." Throndor's head dropped forward. "He claims that he has a way to do real magic. Ovro said he'd kill some Lady Celia and take the soul forge for himself. I thought him crazy, but he paid good gold, so I followed."

The whole time, I'd thought Throndor was a Norn leader, but a mercenary? What was Ovro playing at? He positioned himself as Everard's usurper and the leader of a new society. How did magic fit into any of this?

Throndor's hand had moved from his injury and into a pouch on his belt.

"Get your hand—"

The big man pulled his hand free and stabbed a metal syringe into his thigh. His head rocked back as his skin flushed red. I stepped back, readying the fire to finish him off. Before I could release the flame, the Norn lunged forward and grabbed me by the throat. His momentum drove me back against the workbench. Pieces of metal and tools bounced from the force of the collision. My back protested as the Norn's weight pressed against me, bending me like a horseshoe against an anvil's horn.

I raked his face with the climbing spikes on my hand, but he batted it away, ignoring the tears in his flesh and the blood that ran down his face. He looked like a demon from the underworld with the blood and shadows dancing around him.

"What—?" I gasped. His grin widened as he pressed harder against my throat. My muscles screamed as the pain increased, and my breath became labored as my body fought for air.

He put his face directly in front of mine. "Ovro's serum makes you forget the pain for a bit, but by the time it wears off you'll be dead."

I pulled my left arm between us and triggered the shield. It flashed into view for a moment before it failed, but it did loosen Throndor's grip enough for one breath before the vise returned. He grabbed my left arm and slammed it against the bench, holding it out of the way.

A piece of metal bounced harmlessly against my right hand where I fought for leverage to break free. When Throndor drove me into the bench a second time, it bounced close enough to grab. My vision narrowed to a single point as I forced my mechanical arm to do one last thing before I blacked out. With all the effort I could muster, I drove the piece of metal at the Norn.

The pressure on my throat relaxed and air flooded back into my starved lungs. I wretched as Throndor staggered back from me, hands in front of him. I fought for control of my injured body, knowing I couldn't delay and let the giant get more serum; I'd used everything I had in this fight. Any longer and I'd have joined my friends in the afterlife.

I pushed up from the workbench I'd been leaning on. Throndor slumped against the opposing one, head down, blood dripping like rain off a tree. I crossed to him and pushed him around so I could see his face.

Throndor looked down and went slack-jawed as he saw the metal spike protruding from his chest. I grabbed the metal and unleashed the rest of the stored energy in the alarium cell as lightning. His body convulsed as the smell of charred meat reached my nose. I let the power run until the Norn's hair burst into flames. He dropped to his knees, then fell forward, and I jammed the spike completely through his stilled chest before placing him on the coal forge and burning his body. There wouldn't be another resurrection.

Throndor had told me the most important piece of information without realizing it: Usorin was a distraction, which meant that I'd been sent away from the true target.

Ovro was after the Treetop Workshop.

17

The billowing smoke told me I was too late, though I'd expected it, knowing that Throndor had been another trap laid out to remove me from the board like an errant pawn. I rode the horse into the barn and tied him off, still saddled. Walden Ovro would be gone, and on his way to fulfilling his master plan.

I went through the cabin to the lift, but the door refused to open. I wondered if Roland had blown the couplings or if Walden had destroyed it. It didn't matter. I'd come back to nurse my wounds and regroup with Roland. Maybe the Master Artificer would have a plan, since mine hadn't worked and had gotten all my friends killed in the process. I'd rather lose my arm again than deal with what I'd seen in Bradenbridge.

The door had an override to manually release the locks. Once it stood open, I climbed the cage and followed the ladder to Treetop. As I pushed open the upstairs door, I knew it was bad news. Jabber lay face-down off to the right surrounded by debris. I moved into the room, not caring if

Walden waited for me. After everything I'd lost, my life wasn't overly important.

There wasn't a mark on the butler, which surprised me. With an ungodly amount of effort, I managed to flip him onto his side. His monocle and nose were cracked from hitting the floor, but he appeared to be intact. I opened his charging panel and set my finger against the metal lead. I released a trickle of energy, which his battery absorbed. I reactivated him after a short time had passed.

It would take a bit for him to return to his normal, chatty self, so I surveyed the damage. The main part of the workshop had been rummaged through. Pieces and parts of various projects were strewn across the floor, and the door to the main workshop had been blown from the hinges; the wood was cracked and blackened where the door had once been. The room itself had been set on fire and the windows had burst at some point, leaving bits of paper flapping around in the breeze, but the overhead water reservoirs had done their job. Each section of the workshop held specially made, soft metal pipes. If a fire broke out, the metal melted at a low temperature and the water would extinguish the flames. Grooves in the flooring acted as conduits to remove the extra water to avoid flooding the whole of the structure.

I stepped over pieces of the wreckage, looking for anything that was important or salvageable. Images of Ruari's burned-off hands crept into my thoughts. I needed to focus, but my mind kept returning to the smithy and my dead friends.

My eyes wandered around the room. What a waste. Design drawings, schematics, and books collected from around the world were torn, burnt, or water-logged. Decades of work ruined, and for what?

Roland still hadn't made an appearance and that concerned me, though the old artificer had survived for a long time without my help. I'd have to check the bolt holes to see if he still hid in one of them.

Reaching the far end of the room, I noticed the safe stood untouched. I'd thought this would have been Walden's target; it held the devices, working prototypes, and a large supply of alarium. There was enough gear in there to arm a small magi army. I entered the combination twice, since I'd lost track of the numbers the first try. The door swung open, revealing the storage racks neatly arranged and nothing out of place.

"Master Quinn," a voice said from the doorway. I spun toward it, arm extending, before I realized it was Jabber. "Master Quinn, Roland needs your help."

I swung the safe door closed and spun the dial. No sense leaving it open on the off chance that Walden wasn't done here. I strode across the room to Jabber.

"Where is he?"

"Follow me."

The butler turned and walked at his gaited pace toward the living quarters. Roland had locked himself in his room? Not the plan I would have gone with while under attack, but Roland had tricks up his sleeve.

"Oh, no," Jabber said from ahead of me as he turned the corner that led to Roland's room. I pushed past the butler and stopped dead in my tracks. Roland's body hung by his arms at the end of a rope. His face had been severely beaten and his throat cut. Walden hadn't taken any chances this time.

The final blow came when I looked past him and saw the empty space that had housed the alarium core that powered Treetop. Despair rose as I stared at the scene before me. Ovro had killed everyone important to me, stole Roland's greatest invention, and planned to throw Astaria into war or worse.

"Jabber, what happened?" I moved to Roland and untied his arms, catching his body so it didn't fall to the floor.

"Master Roland stayed in the workshop after you left. He told me he had to ready new devices to fight with, but didn't elaborate. I begged him to eat and get some rest, but he refused. You know how focused Master Roland could be."

I picked up Roland's body from the floor, cradling it like a child. Another person, I cared for, dead. My friend and mentor killed by Ovro as some power play. I would finish the mission Roland and I had embarked on and wouldn't rest until I'd killed Walden Ovro.

Sometime later I realized I still sat in the hall rocking Roland's corpse like a new baby. I had to refocus on finishing the mission and avenging my fallen brother. I'd have to bury him, but at least, for now, I could bring him to the workshop; it seemed a fitting place for him to rest. Jabber had been droning on about mundane things as I placed Roland on the main workbench.

"The lift opened unexpectedly, and a man Roland referred to as Ovro entered the domicile. Master Roland's last command was for me to retire. I was unable to recharge overnight. The next morning, I awoke at the usual time, but I found the workshop as you see it. My energy was low, so I waited for you to return. The only thing I did was to retrieve the message from the Arch Magus."

My head shot up. "Message? What message?"

Jabber removed a rolled piece of parchment from his waistcoat pocket, handing it to me. I unfurled the paper and read.

A rriving in Bradenbridge for a meeting with Lord Magus Usorin. Your attendance is required.

. . .

I t listed the date and time below. The date was tomorrow. It was a two-day trip back to Bradenbridge.

"Why didn't you give this to me right away?"

"You did not request correspondences."

"Of course."

Everard would be walking into a trap without knowing it. This was bigger than my losses. I'd failed at everything else, but I couldn't let Roland down. Without Everard, Astaria would be at the mercy of Walden Ovro and whatever he had planned.

Without learning to fly, I'd never make it in time.

"I have to make it to Bradenbridge by tomorrow. If I leave now and ride all night..."

"At an average rate of speed on a horse you will arrive in Willinshire at dawn. You would need another eight hours assuming fresh horses and not needing sleep to make it to Bradenbridge.

"An airship could make the journey easily as its average rate of speed is—"

"Airship?"

I ran out of the workshop to the inoperable lift. I slid down the ladder and across the yard to the barn. The horses whinnied as I entered, but I ignored them. A dirty cloth covered the boat that Roland had joked was teaching him to be a bird. I tugged the cloth, revealing the boat's frame below. In the center, Roland had constructed a simple boiler like the one Ruari had designed for Usorin's furnace. Attached to a spout hung a limp pile of black material.

Roland had built an airship.

The airship sat on a carriage assembly with wheels. I pushed on the back, but it wouldn't budge. Taking a collar from the tack board, I hooked up one of the horses and rolled the airship to the clearing beyond the shack. I returned the horse to his stall, wondering if I should set them free before I left. If I died, no one knew they were out here.

Returning to the airship, or what would have to pass for one, I set to making it air-worthy. The alarium source stood empty, which didn't surprise me, since leaving a charged boiler around wasn't a great idea. I removed two of the alarium cannisters from my reserves and fit them into place. Heat rose from the boiler as I worked to lay out the balloon so it would inflate properly. I found the mooring ropes and secured the airship to the ground. I needed to return to the workshop and didn't need to return to find the airship was gone.

Next, I attached the wings and guiding mechanism. Roland had built a drive shaft to turn a blade at the ship's rear. In theory, it would propel the craft faster and allow the pilot to steer. At least it did on the big dirigibles that took passengers.

I double-checked the water levels and ascended the ladder back to the workshop. Jabber met me at the entrance.

"Sir, how shall I proceed?"

In essence, Jabber was asking about his existence. Like the horses without food, the butler would cease to operate without alarium charging his circuits.

"I'm going to retrieve the alarium core. Once I return with it, you'll be able to self-charge again," I said.

His face didn't change like mine would, but his tone carried the loss he felt. "If you would be so kind as to shut down my systems, I would rather avoid taking any more damage when my charge fails."

I guided Jabber to a seat. He sat rigid like the proper butler. "Goodnight, Jabber."

"Goodnight, Master Quinn. Fare thee well."

I switched off his power, watching as the light dimmed in his eyes. I'd thought I'd lost everything, but there were still those who depended on my success. It wasn't much, but it was something.

The safe yielded replacement alarium and two bombs. I hadn't had time to replace the bomb I'd used in Cheim, so they would have to do. Most of the devices I hadn't seen before, so no sense in bringing items I didn't know how to operate. I locked up and returned to the barn. The horses nickered as I entered. I fed them each some sugar and led them out to the hitching post. After tying them off with a course rope, I brought them water and grain. If I didn't return, they could chew through the ropes and be free. If I did return, I'd have the horses to help me rebuild.

Steam billowed off the boiler as I approached the airship, which was a good sign. I stepped over the rail and moved the metal spout into place over the boiler. When I opened the valve, the balloon began to fill. The fabric billowed out slowly as the hot air filled the empty space. I watched as the filled balloon pulled the ship off the wheels and floated above the ground, bumping to a stop as the mooring ropes went taut.

No time like the present. I released the ropes and rose smoothly into the air. Using the rudder to steer, I engaged the drive shaft, and the craft lurched forward toward Bradenbridge and my meeting with Walden Ovro.

Only one of us would survive the next meeting. I wondered who it would be.

18

I t took all night to fly to Bradenbridge. Just before the sun rose, I found a clearing to the west of Usorin's keep. I deflated the balloon and made my way to the keep. The meeting was hours off, but I had to be inside prior to Everard's arrival. If I could find and eliminate Walden before he put the Arch Magus in danger, so much the better.

I stalked through the trees, alert for anything out of place. Walden would be expecting me, but the abandoned ventilation ducts gave me a way in; hopefully one he didn't know existed. Nothing moved as I approached the blasted furnace. I would have liked to have made sure I was alone, but the sun had started to crest and the keep was coming to life.

Staying low, I climbed up to the wooden ducts. It would be a snug fit, but I would make it. I removed the rest of the boards, dropping them behind the firebox. With some effort and more lost skin, I pulled myself into the close quarters of the duct.

The going was slow, but the carpenters had built the ducts solidly, so while they creaked a bit, the structure held. Flat on my chest, I pulled myself along toward the first junction that led to the pantry behind the kitchen. I moved along faster once I reached the place where the shaft went through the wall of the keep, where the support was stronger.

After opening the small door they'd installed to access the ducts, I peered down into the darkness of the pantry. The room was at least twenty feet long and half as wide. Not a soul moved, though I could hear the kitchen staff working. I gripped the edge of the opening and lowered myself down until I dropped to the floor below. The door would have to stay open, but I doubted it would raise an alarm.

I moved to the door and peeked out. One of the servants stood with their back to me, talking to someone I couldn't see. This was the best chance I'd get. Moving as quietly as possible, I made my way to the servant's quarters.

Voices floated to me as the keep's staff started their day. Food needed to be prepared and served, chamber pots emptied, and rooms cleaned. I ducked into a stairwell going down, knowing the lower levels would be unoccupied this early in the day. The stairwell was dim, but with my mask I could see enough to avoid falling down the stairs. I reached the door and cracked it open.

There were no guards in the dining chamber. I stepped out and ducked below the table's edge, making my way along the side wall to the doorway. I crouched, ear pressed against the door. Loud voices boomed from outside. I wondered if they'd reported the open hatch in the pantry. The bits and pieces I caught made it sound like they were searching for someone. I needed to move before they found me. I wasn't sure if they'd believe that I was a Watch guard with Roland dead.

Standing, ready to retrace my steps, I felt the sharp stick of a needle in my back.

"So nice of you to join us," was the last thing I heard.

I woke to a hard strike across the jaw. Walden Ovro's face swam in front of my eyes as I tried to get them to focus. The walls, ceiling, and floor were all stone. Chains had been affixed to the walls and a massive machine took up the middle of the room. If I had to guess, I was in the dungeon.

"Ah, there you are," Walden remarked with his normal, acidic humor. "I didn't want you to miss the final move in our fascinating game."

I pushed myself forward, ready to kill him. Ropes bound me to the chair I sat in. My right arm was missing. The shock must have shown on my face because Ovro laughed.

"Missing something, are we?" He held up my mechanical arm. "Quinn, you do beautiful work. I'd commission something, but you'll be dead soon. I guess death is going around."

I bucked against the ropes, again to no avail. "I'll kill you."

He shook his head, a sad look on his face.

"No, you won't. I will say, it impressed me that you killed Throndor. He was a nasty bit of work. If it makes you feel better, I didn't tell him to kill your friends." He pointed off to my left. "Truly, I wanted you to kill that piece of garbage, but we can't have everything, now, can we?"

I followed his gaze to the man huddled next to me. Usorin. His hair was a mess and his eye was badly swollen. He whimpered as I looked at him.

"You wanted me to kill Usorin?" I asked.

He flipped his hand theatrically. "I thought it only fitting that I reward you for making all of this possible. Unfortunately, our Usorin didn't withstand my questioning well. I fear I have broken his delicate mind in the process. Anyway, you had to be away from Treetop so I could get the last piece I needed."

"The alarium core."

"Yes, the alarium core. I hated to kill old Roland, but you shouldn't leave your things lying about where they can get killed." He cocked his head mockingly at me. "If only the man had been reasonable, he'd be alive."

I struggled against the ropes, but I wasn't going anywhere. Behind him stood a large machine. In the center of two tables stood a metal rod with a large gem affixed to it. At the head, I could see the alarium core hooked to a series of devices.

A body laid on the table to the left. The right table was empty.

"What is the device for?"

He clapped excitedly. "I thought you'd never ask. Everard has something I want—real magic. This device will transfer his power to the prismatic orb," he gestured at the large gem, "then into my body. At that point, no one will stand against me. And all of it is thanks to you, Quinn."

Everard hadn't moved since I'd noticed him.

"Is Everard dead?"

"No, he arrived last night for a feast and his food didn't agree with him, so he's sleeping it off."

Usorin cried a bit behind me, but I ignored him. "Is this so you can rule the world?"

"Quinn, you have no idea the stakes of this game, but it is time to finish it once and for all." He moved to the back of the device and a loud whirring noise filed the room. The orb glowed with a blueish light that made strange shadows on the dungeon walls.

I felt a tug on my left arm. Usorin, the man who had cut my arm off in a fit of anger, stared at me with panicked eyes.

"Are you the boy I maimed?" His voice shook like that of an elderly man. His eyes were unfocused and darted around. There was no sign of the Usorin who'd threatened Crimshaw back in the forge.

"Yes."

"I'm so sorry. I didn't think the alarium would destroy the furnace. I should have listened to Ruari." He reached out to touch my missing arm. I jerked back and his hand retreated. "Ovro is going to kill me."

"He's going to kill us all."

I said it to no one, as Usorin had crawled behind my chair. Ovro crossed to stand before me, ignoring the whimpering Lord Magus as he cringed behind my chair.

"I am very vexed that you killed Throndor." He pulled at my ropes, making sure I was secure. "I'd trained him to run the machine, but now I have to do it myself."

I laughed in his face. "No miracle machine to bring him back?"

He slapped me. "You burnt his body, you ignorant dolt. I will make sure your death is exquisitely painful once I possess Everard's magic."

He spun on his heel and went to Everard's side. Tubes ran from the Arch Magus' temples. He wasn't strapped down, which surprised me, but then again, he wasn't awake. After a bit, Ovro climbed onto the table and attached a series of tubes to himself before reaching over and pulling a rope he'd affixed to his table.

The machine grew louder, and the light pulsed within the orb as it went. The rope fell to the ground next to the table and Ovro released it. I watched as the energy crackled along the metal rod that ended in the prismatic orb. There was nothing left to do but watch, and, well, die.

Usorin's face appeared before me.

"If I free you, will you save me?" He didn't wait for an answer; he sawed at the ropes with a knife. In a matter of moments, I was free, but how to stop Ovro? My arm lay on the floor by his table, but it would take too long to reattach, and I didn't know how long I had until the transfer was complete. I stayed out of Walden's field of vision while I thought. I could pull the plug on the alarium core, but would it matter now that the orb pulsed blue with new energy? If the magic had gone that far, shutting off the machine would only delay the inevitable.

Running to the machine, I did the only thing I could think of: I grabbed the prismatic orb and pulled.

That's when things spun out of control.

19

Energy coursed through me as my hand closed on the orb. I strove to pull it free of the metal setting, but I didn't have enough leverage to move it with only one arm. The power intensified as I fought to break the contact between Everard and Ovro. If I didn't succeed, Ovro would own the magic that kept the people of Astaria safe from the Norns and other warrior-led nations. I redoubled my efforts.

The orb broke free with a loud crack, sending me sprawling across the stones. I maintained my grip on the crystal sphere, clutching it to my chest. Ovro screamed in rage as he realized the transfer had stopped.

Lights swirled around me in a chaotic pattern as I clung to the orb. The energy flowed over me as if I stood in the center of a great waterfall. Colors beyond description danced before my eyes, drawing patterns that eluded my understanding. Shimmering notes of music teased at the edge of my hearing.

The room around me vanished as I began to accelerate upwards and away from my body, which laid on the floor.

My eyes, now lifeless, rolled back into my head. I wanted to see what happened, but I could no longer see the room I'd been in. Before me rose a field covered in an icy-blue glow. As the landscape grew, details became apparent. A lattice-work of ice covered the entirety of the space. Motes of light drifted up from the ice, spinning and dancing as they floated away on an unfelt breeze.

"It is beautiful, is it not?" a female voice asked from beside me. The woman wore a blue robe stitched with elaborate symbols running its length. They were the same symbols from the Guard's robes. I couldn't see her face for the hood.

"It is. May I ask what its purpose is?"

She nodded. "This is the soul forge where all things begin and end. I have need of you, Quinn."

I swallowed hard.

"What may I do for you, my Lady Celia?"

I should have been afraid, or at least concerned, but a wave of peacefulness rode over me like the heat from the alarium forge.

"You have a choice to make. If you choose the path I lay out before you, there will be pain, suffering, and death. If you falter, you will be broken and tormented for all time. Walk away from this path and you will be free to live out your life."

She turned away from me as if she studied the expanding landscape beyond us. "Forces move against the people of Astaria. You may live a happy life, have children, and grow old, or Ovro might obtain his goal and all might die. Know that another will rise if you walk away. There is no shame in it. Will you choose duty or happiness?"

I looked down to where my arm had been. I'd lost so much and to serve her would mean losing more. Ruari's voice echoed in the back of my head: *The path will always become clear in time. Be happy Quinn, for who knows what tomorrow brings.*

Could I just walk away? I could leave Astaria with my metal arm, find a place to settle down and be the blacksmith I was meant to be. Would Emma, or any other woman, be happy with a one-armed man? Even with my mechanical arm, my self-worth suffered. I'd barely stopped Ovro, and then only through my own ignorance.

I studied the woman before me. I couldn't see her face, but her dark hair spilled down the front of her robes. Her hands were held contentedly before her. Nothing about her spoke of violence or malice toward me, though looks could be deceiving. Dark metal could still be hot as it cooled.

I'd lost everyone important to me because I'd let Ovro know who I was. He might hunt me down to exact his revenge, and I'd be powerless to stop it with Treetop in shambles and Roland dead. Was I strong enough to defeat Ovro? He'd ambushed Everard, who'd had the magic for longer than I'd been alive. Could I do better? Did I even want to try?

I pictured a forge of my own, my wife taking care of the children in the background. I could be happy; have a family the fates had robbed me of. No more loneliness. The scene shifted to Ruari's forge and the dead bodies.

The path rose up before me and I knew I would walk it, no matter the cost.

"I will serve."

A jolt struck me as my vision collapsed to a single point. With a mighty explosion, the vision grew until I could feel every soul that had made up the forge before me. These were my wards and I would protect them.

"You are in possession of the soul forge's magic. Will you use it wisely to defend the alarium from those who would destroy it?"

"Who would want to destroy alarium?" I blurted out.

"Alarium holds magic. If the alarium is destroyed, the

magic will fade, and your world will plunge into darkness. Evil beings such as the one you call Ovro desire the darkness, for it hides their evil."

"But he was stealing Everard's magic."

"Incorrectly, he thought the magic would destroy the alarium. With the magic you carry, you will be my champion and must destroy Ovro before he can accomplish his goals. Serve me well."

I knelt before her. "Of course."

Her hand touched my head and the power surged, growing until I thought I might burst. Then it was gone. I opened my eyes and saw I was back in the dungeon. Usorin sat in the corner, rocking back and forth. I searched for Ovro, but he wasn't there.

Everard sat looking befuddled as I took to my feet. Our eyes locked. "She has given the magic to you."

I nodded, not trusting myself to speak.

Everard, Arch Magus of Astaria, bowed his head to me. "Welcome, Arch Magus Quinn."

And that is how I became a wizard.

THE END

< < < < > > > >

ACKNOWLEDGMENTS

Somehow I've managed to write three books. What started out as proving to myself I could finish a book has turned into somewhat of an obsession. I'm very fortunate to have people around me who are supportive and kind, and listen to me ramble about the made up people in my head.

This book is the culmination of a lot of talented people working on a story that got stuck in my brain until I finally wrote the damn thing. Victoria Loder edited the draft into a polished piece. It took a bit of rewriting, but the changes she suggested took this from good to great. YMMV. My old mischief making buddy, Angela Bridges, aka "Ms. Thang", did the copy edits and proof reading to make sure all the poor grammar and typos were removed, though I may have introduced a few when I added just a couple more things after she finished. John Hartness did the eBook and paperback layouts.

They always say don't judge a book by its cover, but I'll forgive you if you do in this case. I'd wanted to work with Natania Barron because I love her cover art and she did not disappoint. She took my request for a metal armed black-smith and made it into a beautiful cover.

Normally, I have a crew of people who beta read my books, but Chuck, Jon, and Cheri jumped in to read this one and, as always, gave incredible feedback.

I'd also be remiss if I didn't thank Dr. Juan Gloria and the staff at Carolinas Chiropractic and Spinal Rehab for continually fixing my bad shoulder so I can write. Without them, I doubt I'd have gotten through writing this book.

Our new puppy Blaze has finally settled into being my writing buddy, lying in my lap or at my feet while I write into the night. He's been a lot of fun and full of energy.

Lastly, I have to thank my incredibly wonderful and supportive family. They put up with the long hours of my writing, listen to story ideas, agent rejections, and travel around to attend cons where I do panels and sell books. Emily and Nicholas have stuck by me through a lot of tough spots and continue to be an inspiration to me. They work hard and are (usually) so easy to parent and love me no matter how many times I crack Dad jokes. My wife Hope deserves a huge thank you. Not only does she pick up the slack when I disappear for weeks on end to finish a book, but she reads and edits the first draft of everything I write. She's my rock, my best friend, and the most amazing woman I know, and I lucked out when she agreed to spend her life with me.

ABOUT THE AUTHOR

About the Author Patrick Dugan was born in the far north of New York, where the cold winds blow. This meant lots of time for reading over the long winters. His parents didn't care what he read as long as he did and thus Patrick started with a steady diet of comics and science fiction novels.

His debut novel, Storm Forged, Book One of the Darkest Storm series, was published by Falstaff Books in May of 2018. Unbreakable Storm followed in 2019. Book 3 is scheduled for May of 2020.

When you start out as an author, nobody tells you about all of the other "jobs" that you take on in addition to writing novels. Being a full time technologist has led Patrick to start a blog on the uses of writing technologies and how to apply them to the writing process. He delves into software, hardware, social media, and all things web related.

Patrick resides in Charlotte, NC with his wife, two children, and wild dog Blaze. In his limited spare time, he's a gamer, homebrewer, and DIYer.

You can find out more at www.patrickdugan.net

Made in the USA
Columbia, SC
13 August 2021

42941422R00079